Modern Romances

STORIES

BY

JUDY LOPATIN

NEW YORK *Fiction Collective* BOULDER

1986

First Edition
First Printing, 1986

"Retrospective on Weegee" and "The Real Life of Viviane Ro-
mance" originally appeared in *Mississippi Review*; "Etiology
of the New War," "Modern Romances," and "Nuit Blanche"
originally appeared in *Benzene*; "Fast and Loose, A Historical
Romance" originally appeared in *Diana's Almanac*; and "The
Mystery of Madame Kitten" originally appeared in *Zone*.
"Trixie Taylor, Hospital Nurse" originally appeared in *Shiny
International*.

Published by Fiction Collective with assistance from the National Endowment for the Arts; with the support of the Pub-
lications Center, University of Colorado, Boulder; and with
the cooperation of Brooklyn College, Illinois State University,
and Teachers & Writers Collaborative.

Grateful acknowledgement is also made to the Graduate
School, the School of Arts and Sciences, and the President's
Fund of the University of Colorado, Boulder.

Library of Congress Cataloging-in-Publication Data

Lopatin, Judy.
      Modern romances and other stories.

      I. Title.
PS3562.0665M63   1986   813'.54   86-7711
ISBN 0-932-51102-3
ISBN 0-932-51103-1 (pbk.)
Manufactured in the United States of America

Designed by Abe Lerner
Typeset by Fisher Composition Inc.

For Mom and Dad

CONTENTS

Romance: A medieval tale in verse or prose based on legend, chivalric love and adventure, or the supernatural;

a prose narrative treating imaginary characters involved in events remote in time or place and usually heroic, adventurous, or mysterious;

a love story; a class of such literature;

something that lacks basis in fact;

an emotional attraction or aura belonging to an especially heroic era, adventure, or calling;

a passionate love affair.

Romance DEFINED BY WEBSTER'S.

Modern Romances

NEW WAVE MOVIE: LOVE SCENE

LUCIE ET GUY walking along the street. Guy stopping and pushing her against the gate of a storefront.

—I love you, don't you realize that.

I've refused princesses. Don't you know what that means, you jerk, when I say I love you—

(Shaking her, grabbing her by her hair, yanking it)

—I love you, I love you.

(Then:)

—I know what it is. You have something that I've never seen in another woman.

Lucie (lightly): But I'm not a woman. I'm just a girl. . . .

Guy: I realize what it is now. It's . . . that cross between FEAR and VIOLENCE.

Lucie gives him a look that means: please be careful with me.

NEW WAVE MOVIE: SEX SCENE

At Guy's place. Under the covers naked. Rubbing against each other. Lucie urging him: Finger me, Guy. Harder.

Guy protesting: These are not just any fingers.

9

Lucie: I'll do it myself then.
He won't let her. Holding her down he murmurs:
—You look like a little demented Cleopatra.

CHARACTER OF OUR HEROINE

Lucie is a New Wave singer and guitarist. Who (never) reveals herself in her actions and the stories she tells about herself.

PASSION

Lucie met Guy (for example) at Village Oldies. They talked about music. They had the same tastes, only he knew everything about every record ever made. He told her he played guitar, she told him she wrote songs.

Idyll in Washington Square Park: she played for him, he read her poetry aloud to her.

The first day (it was day) she went to Guy's apartment, he told her he didn't like women and hadn't liked them in 4 years. Women, he thought, and told her so, were stupid. Lucie shocked him because she wasn't (stupid). Also, he didn't like sex. Lucie agreed: I can see how it bores you. But anyway, somehow, they did fuck that night. She says it was pretty good. There was blood on the wall. She doesn't know how it got there. He must've wiped his hand on the wall after fingering her.

That was the only time they ever fucked, though since then they've slept together.

That was not the first time Lucie saw the blood on the wall. At a rock club, she met a lead vocalist who stood at the back of the stage, yelling in a raincoat. Between sets they ducked into the ladies' room and he fucked her with a beer bottle. She didn't feel a thing, but out came the blood.

Together they smeared it on the wall.

10

FIDELITY

Guy used to live with another guy, called Roger. That was the summer Lucie met them. Then the arrangements changed: Roger moved out to live with a girl, and another girl (Laura) moved in with Guy, on a more or less platonic basis ("Guy didn't want to fuck her"). Lucie likes one story that was told to her:

One time Laura came home after Lucie had been over. Lucie and Guy had been lying on the couch (daybed). Laura wanted to know how come there was gum on the sheets. Guy said he'd bought some gum that day. Laura said: Oh yeah? What brand?

Then she said: What's that new cologne you have that smells like orange blossoms? Come here and smell these sheets.

And all Guy (caught) could say was Uh-oh.

TEEN IDOL

Fear and violence, continued.

Quoting Guy, Lucie is reminded of The Man She Knew in Buffalo.

When she was 15 and waiting for the bus near a porno-house, a man offered her a ride home. He asked her if she wanted to make some money. Lucie said yes, if it wouldn't involve sex.

He agreed. He only liked sex if it was imaginative. He liked stories. Lucie said she could tell him stories. He said he'd pay her $50 if she could tell him a good story.

Over a period of two or three months, in three or four or five storytelling sessions, Lucie told him stories about ripping little girls' thighs apart with pliers until they bled. About him fucking her mother in the ass. Him killing her sisters. (This because she was supposed to hate them and be jealous of them. Just a story.)

11

Things The Man wanted Lucie to do for him: Eat cigarette butts. Lick car tires. Play with pliers on her tits and lick them. Things he wanted to do to Lucie: Spit in her face. Things Lucie refused to do: Eat out ashtrays, piss on him.

The Man would call at her house to arrange their meetings. Lucie told her mother he was a filmmaker. He was. He made porn movies. He had fliers he sold to soldiers at Fort Dix for $10 each. He wanted to make up a flier featuring Lucie alone, a whole portfolio of pictures. In addition wanted her to pose for a magazine he had—the kind with American girls' pictures in the magazines distributed in Europe, and European girls in the American issues. So no one would recognize them.

Lucie hated it when he spit on her. Thick, gobby spit. Doing stuff for him wouldn't bother her so much when she was doing it, but the next day she would feel disgusted with herself.

When he spit on her he would say: That's a blockage I have to get out. You have to overcome these blockages.

He also said he hated his mother and he hated women—generally, not personally. He wouldn't hurt Lucie, personally. He told her: I think you're a real nice kid.

He looked like Frankie Valli with pockmarks.

CHEMISTRY

Why Lucie Likes Roger: He appreciates her, puts her on a pedestal. Notices her and compliments her on her lipstick, her nail polish, things other guys take for granted. Likes her sleazy image. Thinks she's sexy. Adores her. Most of all, wants her.

Why People Don't Like Lucie (According to Lucie): She's Too Competitive . . . Has Too Much Energy.

What Roger Must Like: Butyl acetate, toluene, nitrocellulose, ethyl acetate, isopropryl alcohol, formaldehyde resin, dibutyl phthalate, camphor, stearalkonium hectorite, quarternium-18, benzophenone-1, silica, D&C reds #6, #34, #7, iron oxides (ingredients of Lucie's nail polish).

ELECTRA COMPLEX

Lucie reminisces: My father has the nicest cock I ever saw. . . . But he always had this hangnail.

"It was sick—you don't know what it did to me"

"I hated my father for so long"

"Disgusting"

"Somebody has their hands where they're not supposed to"

It started when she was six. She would sleep with her father because she was wetting the bed. Her mother worked nights (a nurse). When he started doing it she would wake up and be too scared to do anything but pretend to be asleep. She stopped sleeping with him. He'd come in to her room and try to do it. When she was about 10 she wouldn't let him.

"Stop, leave your piggish hands off me"

It runs in his family, she says. His brother does it. His brother tried to do it to her (that's how she knows).

POPULARITY

Before: Lucie was precocious, spending one pubescent summer in a black-lit basement room with a nervous breakdown. . . .

After: Lucie has dyed her hair black, because it is fashionable, and/or to cover the gray. Living up to the underground tends to ruin one's bloom of youth.

Everyone, sooner or later, needs Loving Care.

Now Lucie has a steady boyfriend, Spencer, who spanks her.

Lucie's figure before & after: She never eats, but she

13

never loses weight. Before she was popular, somebody called her The Goodyear Blimp (behind her back). Then she bought a pair of sadomasochistic boots with heels high enough to make her look taller and thus thinner.

It is difficult to go out walking much, in such boots, so Spencer brings her her food. If he doesn't, she doesn't eat, but usually he does, and she does, or so at least it seems, since she doesn't lose weight, and thus must not miss many meals.

One advantage of having a steady boyfriend (Lucie admits) is You've Got Someone To Depend On.

GOING STEADY

Steady sex is another such advantage. Besides:

It is oh so suspenseful to sleep with Spencer, because when he wakes up screaming and shaking her in the middle of the night she's sure he's going to kill her. . . .

But it's only a thrill and a chill. Only a delicious taste of death. Because Lucie can depend on her steady.

SIN SUFFER AND REPENT

I break the rules, announces Lucie to all her new boyfriends, it is just as easy to suffer and repent without going to the trouble of sinning.

That is the fun of modern romance, nothing can ever be a terrible mistake, so over and over again you can look over your shoulder and see the arms of your past, see them encircle your waist with comfort so cold you don't feel a thing—

A Phantasm, A Bird—

A PHANTASM. A bird—

Thus the story begins, in a bungalow adrift, with shutters, aluminum siding. . . .

The bungalow is secluded, the woman is by herself by the sea, and one morning she is out bird-watching and she sees the ghost of her past.

The ghost of her past is wearing a white dress. A "dimity frock" they were once called.

They were called "dimity frocks" in a time long before the woman was born, in her present incarnation. So the ghost of her past must be the ghost of her past life.

Now the phantasm in the white dress is flying, pretending to be a bird, though it's not high enough. It's only about five feet above the ground, not even clearing the woman's head. She is afraid that if the phantasm gets too close, it will fly right into her neck, puncturing it— woman and ghost toppling into a bloody heap on the sand.

The woman together with the phantasm on the beach, from here to eternity, and nobody to discover her body. Her husband? No husband. The aluminum siding was put in by professionals. Twenty dollars an hour plus materials, and that was years ago, before the rates went up. But it's weathering well.

17

(Aluminum: a bluish silver white malleable ductile light trivalent metallic element with good electrical and thermal conductivity, high reflectivity. . . .)

The woman sees herself prostrate on the ground, imploring the birdlike phantasm for her right to live—at least until the end of this life.

But then she separates herself out from the phantasm, from the heap, disentangles herself, brushes the sand off, because it's not her ghost after all. It's someone else's ghost, someone who couldn't wound her, someone she wounded. In one of her past lives. A child? A mother? A pet parakeet, perhaps. . . .

The woman laughs at the thought of a nineteenth-century parakeet out to haunt her. A medieval bat is even more preposterous.

The bird, white-feathered, a species she has not come across before, flies up and away. The woman throws the binoculars on the ground. But secretly, that night, comes out to search for them and retrieve them.

2

I wonder what that husband I used to have is doing, the woman wonders.

The time: a Friday afternoon of the present day.

So the husband, or ex-husband, must be in his office in the city. He's writing to his mistress, who is now on a beach, or in a cottage. She shares a cottage with four other people who commute each weekend from Manhattan; only the girl works for an enlightened company that lets its employees out every Friday at noon, so she is on the beach (or in a cottage) while the man is still writing at his desk. She's an ordinary girl, this mistress (unlike the wife), so ordinary in her job, her choice of cottage and island location, her affair with a middle-aged previously-married man. And her perfidy: the girl sleeps with her four roommates in the cottage.

All the woman in the bungalow wanted to know was what her husband was up to, and that mistress of his intrudes and takes it all over. That's the way it is with modern girls, they want to command every situation.

The woman in the bungalow sleeps alone. She goes bird-watching alone. Sometimes she sings. . . .

By the sea, by the sea, a woman watches birds and waits for something to happen.

The mistress on Fire Island (for such is the ordinary island location she has picked for her summer weekends) never waits for things to happen. There isn't time. She can't even see herself getting old, it's all so fast. . . .

Still, now she is only twenty or twenty-two. That is still a girl in this day. The husband doesn't even think of her as a mistress. It's too old-fashioned a word. She is a girlfriend. Anyway a mistress is only what a husband has. Or had.

But if the girl is too young to know what a dimity frock is, the woman is also too young to have *owned* one.

The ex-husband doesn't know the woman, his ex-wife, sleeps alone in a bungalow on a remote and ghostly seaside. Nor does he know that his girlfriend does not sleep alone.

Her roommates number three boys and one girl, and she sleeps with them all. She says: Excuse me if I'm wrong, but it's tough these days, being a single girl in New York.

The woman would say: I like to be alone. I want to be alone. Except she has no one to say it to.

Soon the man, the ex-husband, will be alone also. Already he is stranded in his office, thinking of sunshine but unable to walk out into it. Meanwhile his girlfriend is on Fire Island having her fun, and he is unhappily writing memos at his desk and casting aspersions on the motives of his associates. The letter to his mistress, or girlfriend, is also on his desk, waiting to be sealed with a kiss. Now he mixes them up. Into the interoffice manila envelope, destined for his boss, he deposits his letter of torrid love tempered by misgivings about the future. Into the letter addressed to the girl (at her city address, so it will be there when she comes back to civilization; phones cannot reach her now) he slips the memo to his boss, in which he displays a surly and ungenerous side of his character the girlfriend knows he possesses but pretends not to. She is a great pretender, she is, and a realist.

The story began in a bungalow, floated across unnamed bodies of water to the mainland (Manhattan), took an easily traced path to another shoreline (Fire Island), ferried back to the mainland for a last look at the man writing at his desk. . . . And all these travels took less than an instant, because they all occurred in the same place—inside a bungalow—

The woman in the bungalow has been there since long ago, when she rented the bungalow and contracted for the professional siding men to insulate the house against strong winds and tidal catastrophes.

(Aluminum is one of the Elements. She looked it up in a reference book, found the list: Aluminum, Americium, Antimony, Argon, Arsenic. . . .

She wasn't crying, only dreaming; the words blurred, and she saw things she knew about—not the Elements at all, but aluminum siding, and the American way of life, and alimony, and the quest of the Argonauts in search of the Golden Fleece, all those mythologies; and *Arsenic and Old Lace,* a romantic comedy even she was too young to have seen, when it first appeared, though she catches it often on the late show.)

3

But those were the old days. The woman no longer catches things on the late show. Soon after it gets dark it is time for bed.

The woman thinks: Not only is it the early bird that catches the worm, one has to get up early to watch it happening.

Bird-watching, in the early morning sun, is a healthy thing to do. Her binoculars are the best: scratch-resistant, scientifically ground lenses, so she can hone in with no distortions upon all creatures flying far above her.

The woman has taken good care of her binoculars over the years. It is true that once upon a time they did nothing but sit in their dark pouch warding off dust, in different drawers she had in Manhattan apartments. They were a gift from her husband, after he had already given her a camera, an opera glass, and a fishing rod and reel. Occasionally the opera glass came out of the drawer.

Now the camera and the fishing equipment would come in handy too, but the woman does not like to shoot and fish.

There are some things even a woman alone on an island in the present day hasn't the heart to do.

By the sea, by the sea. . . .

The story doesn't end.

Something is happening to the woman. Her bird-watching is taking a new turn.

She thinks, if I can spot something rare and lovely, it will all be worth it.

Day after day, she sees lovely birds: blue jays and cardinals, every species of the colorful male. But they are not rare.

The woman decides, I want to see a bird so rare that everyone else thinks it is extinct.

What she wants to see is the white-feathered bird of an unknown species, the one that flew dangerously close to the ground, the one that almost hit her in the neck. She is always on the lookout.

Soon she has eyes for nothing but that bird. She leaves her binoculars at home: dimity birds fly dangerously close to the ground. . . . But every white bird she sees is too far away.

Dimity birds are extinct
Dimity birds are extinct
Dimity birds are extinct

At night, in sheets of 100% cotton mercerized for the rigors of the present day, the woman finds flocks and flocks of dimity birds. She catches them by their necks and wrings the life out of them, wrings their souls out, so that the dimity frocks float off to claim bodies in the next life—in somebody else's life. . . .

Sometimes the husband writes her a love-memo, the girlfriend drowns in a sea of bodies on a bed—

When the sun comes up the woman will go walking on the beach, just like any fun-loving girl.

But inside, until morning restores her calm, the aluminum siding vibrates with pleasure, the shutters shudder, the bungalow floats off to sea. . . .

Retrospective on Weegee

1. BIOGRAPHICAL NOTE

ON MANY OCCASIONS Weegee the Famous (Weegee the world-famous blood-and-guts photojournalist) took pictures at movie theaters with his infrared film and flash. In 1945, in 1951, in 1953.

(Weegee sneaks in with his infrared flash and film and takes the picture and they never know it. They are in the dark.)

Readers of the New York tabloids see the pictures and know who took them. Weegee stamps all his pictures on the back, "Credit Weegee the Famous."

Weegee did become famous in 1945 upon publication of his first book, *Naked City*. This diamond-in-the-rough became a high-society darling. Rich women cruised with him each night in the hopes of witnessing a murder. Finally he could stop visiting two-buck whorehouses and get all the women he wanted.

(This was what Weegee was after.

This is what the women who chased with him, chased after him—this is what they were after, besides a murder a night. Says Weegee in his autobiography: they wanted to see what it was like to sleep with a genius.

Were women, in 1945, the pushovers Weegee claims? What about the Standards our mothers, young girls of that time, used to tell us about?

Weegee was (in 1945, even more so in 1951 and 1953) middle-aged, crude, ugly, vulgar. What did women see in him? He often slept in his clothes. Did he smell? He smoked cigars. His cigars must have smelled.)

Weegee is an authority on the scams women without a dime pull. He gives them a few bucks for makeup, they buy some at Woolworth's, and after they fix themselves up they vanish. This in the days before he is really Famous.

In women Weegee sees: pimples under the makeup. His infrared film penetrates beneath the pancake, exposes the terrain. Later, after he is famous, when he turns to trick photography, he sees: multiple breasts, contorted faces.

Weegee grew up poor. His first girl was a sweet gentle thing who did not resist when he pulled her to him on the roof of a tenement building one hot sultry summer night.

(The facts of this encounter and others, if one wants more of them, are in Weegee's autobiography, *Weegee by Weegee*, though the details are often left out.)

Weegee was named after the Ouija Board because people said he was psychic. He was always at the scene of a crime before the cops, sometimes before the crime. Much of the credit for this goes to the police radio in his car.

After receiving messages, Weegee and his Speed Graphic camera traveled fast.

Critics these days appreciate Weegee more as a voyeur than a clairvoyant.

In spite of this, or perhaps because of it, the International Center of Photography held a retrospective of his work in 1977, when (almost ten years after his death) he had been nearly forgotten.

2. PORTRAIT OF THE PHOTOGRAPHER AS A VOYEUR

(1945)

Weegee takes in a matinee at the Palace Theater.

(In 1945 Weegee took pictures of children—half-asleep, picking their noses, whispering secrets and touching—at the Palace Theater. In the special edition commemorating the Weegee retrospective, the cycle of Palace Theater pictures includes one of a couple kissing in an audience watching a 3-D movie. Everyone, except the girl getting kissed, is wearing 3-D glasses which provide them with the depth perspective a 3-D movie requires.

You get the impression, from the book, that this picture—second of five—was also taken in 1945. If, in lumping all the Palace Theater pictures together, the commemorators of the retrospective assumed they were all taken at the same time, that was sloppy scholarship. A little bit of research into 3-D contradicts this easy conclusion. Weegee must have returned to the Palace Theater years later, in 1953. It was not until 1953 that 3-D movies which require special glasses came about. This short-lived phenomenon (short-lived because the glasses were uncom-

27

fortable) was called Natural Vision, which was thought up as a cheaper version of Cinerama, which in turn was thought up to provide thrills that television, the new medium, could not.

So the picture of the 3-D kissers, and the story behind it, does not happen until Weegee is well-experienced as a movie-theater voyeur.)

Weegee comes to the Palace Theater for a matinee.

(Where is the Palace Theater? Does it matter? It does not matter if the theater still exists, though that does not keep me from wondering anyway. Also, what movie were they watching?)

The matinee in 1945 at the Palace Theater is (must be) a kiddie picture. The place is filled with children. It must not be a very good movie, either, since the children are not paying it much attention.

In fact, many of the children are looking around them. Of these, some see Weegee. While it is true that his flash does not go off in a burst of light, the camera itself is not invisible. Nor is Weegee, who is not a big man by adult standards, but who is still pretty big, to a kid.

Weegee has to feel out of place. He has been running around the city since midnight, on the prowl for fires and murders, and whatever exhilaration they provided is beginning to wear off. He is not ready to go home. He is too tired to go to a whorehouse. In fact, he is just in the matinee to sleep a little.

But this is probably not true. In the first place, kiddie matinees—at least those of my day—are notorious for their noise. (Though the pictures he took show the kiddies themselves looking more or less soporific.) In the second place, Weegee is known to have almost boundless energy, or at least the kind of zeal that keeps one wide awake at obscure nocturnal hours. If anything, Weegee is only jaded. He is tired of murders, murders, murders, though he is thankful for them because they sell. And by now, he is comfortable with them. Actually, beneath the bluster, Weegee is a shy man. It helps that, at a murder, half-conscious victims and loved ones crazed with grief barely notice his presence. Not to mention bystanders who would rather watch the murder, the dying victims, the craziness of grief and police sirens.

So Weegee walks into a matinee with his camera and thinks, Maybe I can take some nice pictures for a change.

Maybe he thinks back on his early career and the children he made his living on. In his early days as a street freelancer, he bought a pony and went around taking pictures of Lower East Side children posed atop the pony. Then he would develop the pictures and, at week's end, make the rounds of the parents. They always found money to spare for the pleasure of seeing and displaying their children—city children, poor children—on a pony. They could not resist. It was the pony they were after. When Weegee lost the pony to his creditors, he was out of business. He tried a toy car, but nobody went for it.

With these memories in mind, Weegee sits next to a little girl. She is about ten, with a pure complexion. (She is too young for pimples.) She is leaning back in her chair, her lids almost closed.

Can you imagine the tension in the air? That is, the degree of tension—taking as a given fact that there *was* tension in the air, no need to imagine it. On the other hand, since it is not a given fact (it is not a recorded fact), maybe it is only imagining to begin with.

Weegee knows the little girl is pure. (This might be a cause of the tension. If there is any tension, it is sexual, and has nothing to do with the fact that at one time he photographed little children on top of ponies.) For one thing, she is very young. Also, he has been around prostitutes and other tough babes enough to know women. Enough to tell what kind of women little girls will become. Or maybe he only thinks he knows. As he told a newspaper editor once (the editor, bored with photos of dead gangsters, advised Weegee to put some sex in his pictures): the only women he knows are hookers, pickpockets and shoplifters. And when you think about it, if this is the case—and no doubt it is, since the society women only come later, after *Naked City*—then Weegee only knows about a certain *kind* of woman. The kind that have grown up to be hookers, pickpockets and shoplifters. He might be able to recognize these in their early childhood, but there are many other types he would not recognize, unless you divide (unless Weegee divides) women into only two categories, hooker/pickpocket/shoplifter and non-hooker/pickpocket/shoplifter.

Also, does he realize some women start out quite pure, stay pure for a while and then end up just the opposite? Weegee, simple man that he is, does not bother with ambiguities. He takes his pictures with black-and-white high-contrast film. The critics call it expressionism.

Expressionism is well-suited to the gaudy horror that is murder, not so well-suited to capturing a dreamy face and the thoughts behind it.

The little girl is trying to dream in the movie. She probably *is* dreaming. It is only Weegee who thinks that this is no longer possible, who believes that sound has destroyed the magic of the movies. More egotism. Weegee used to play the violin accompaniment to silent movies, he used to move the audience to tears. Now, he no longer has that power. So he thinks there is no more escape, in the movies, because there is too much noise, too much talk.

But the little girl is dreaming. She is not paying any attention to Weegee.

(Could Weegee imagine her as his child? No, because he cannot imagine himself married.)

He thinks, If I take her picture, it will spoil her.

The things he takes pictures of now are ugly.

(Does he realize that?)

Finally, ultimately, necessarily for any dramatic interest—the little girl feels his eyes on her. Or else she sees him out of the corner of her eye. She turns to look at him.

Weegee won't want to destroy the scene. He doesn't say a word. He wants to pull out his camera and shoot her, but he resists. He hopes she won't say anything.

She says, Mister, will you take my picture?

Now, it is not that Weegee does not take pictures of people just for fun. In fact, at his summer nudist camp, he organized a camera club and photographed nudist weddings, bar mitzvahs, all the parties. He could just as well think of those people who clamored to have their pictures taken. But instead, he remembers a drowning at Coney Island five years earlier. A young man was dragged out of the water—dead or perhaps only unconscious. Nobody knew yet. Spectators were mesmerized. Ambulances came running with a doctor to resuscitate the swimmer—naturally, an impossible job if he was already dead, but possible—if not probable—if his future had not yet become his past. (I would like to linger longer on questions of resuscitating what's dead, and what's dead, but this is not relevant to the scene from *Weegee's* point of view, or to the scene itself, which (from Weegee's point of view) is meant to illuminate the encounter he might have had with the pure little girl.)

Enter Weegee, there at the scene to capture it as usual—a moment of high drama. But just as he snaps the picture, the drowned man's bathing-beauty girlfriend unexpectedly looks up, and, in the face of disaster, smiles her prettiest for the camera.

(If Weegee is reminded of this scene, he is reminded of women who only want him for his money, later for his genius. Women who are quicker than a Speed Graphic.)

Weegee gets up and goes to the men's room. When he gets back, he chooses a seat a few rows ahead of the little girl. (Will she be waiting for him to come back? Will she wonder why he has moved away and left her? Does Weegee wonder all this?) He waits a few minutes before he dares to turn to watch her. She is again slumped back in her seat, watching the movie and dreaming. She is again unaware of him. So he shoots.

After the picture is developed, it turns out the child behind the little girl had been picking its nose. That becomes the reason the picture was taken.

That may have been what happened. Or, Weegee may have been in those days a nicer man than I think.

(1951)

Six years later, Weegee gets an assignment from the editor of a magazine called *Brief* to get some pictures of people eating, sleeping, and making love in movie theaters.

(In this section—in this time period—we know more facts, so we have less to imagine, though the facts in themselves are juicier than in the 1945 pure-child fantasy. We even get a clue, in the autobiography, as to Weegee's thoughts and feelings, though it is hard to know how to take his tone. He might only be kidding when he talks about realism and emotion.)

"Weegee," the editor says, "get some pictures of people doing everything in a movie theater they do in the outside world—eating, sleeping, making love."

So Weegee goes to the all-night movie theaters in Times Square, which might or might not be as seedy as they are now. (Were they as seedy? The question does not exactly depend on whether or not "making love" meant actual sexual intercourse or just kissing and fooling around, but knowing the meaning of this euphemism in that time and place would help us to understand the time and place better.

The time and place, we know, is 1951 and a Times Square movie theater.)

33

Weegee has no trouble getting the pictures of eating and sleeping. Lovemaking is another question.

It isn't as though he would have disturbed anyone. He got the movie theater manager's OK. Weegee demonstrated his famous infrared film and flash, which shoots without warning, but also without light. (See *Weegee's Secrets of Shooting with Photo Flash*, 1953.)

As long as nobody's disturbed and can go on with their pleasures, what's the harm? Weegee and the manager agree.

So Weegee sneaks into one of the boxes—in the balcony—sets up a camera, aims it at the audience, and waits. And listens. And when he hears a groan or a sigh, he pushes the button. (Play-by-play in *Weegee by Weegee*.) This was his first approach, and it didn't work. But why was it his first approach?

(The problem of psychological tone follows.)

Weegee claims, "I pride myself on reality. Even in a movie theater. I wanted the love to be real, to come right from the heart and soul. I didn't want it to be a casual pickup, a one-night stand."

(How can we believe that? What does Weegee know about love from the heart and soul? What has that to do with what goes on in the dark in an all-night movie on West 42nd Street? Granted, most of those who neck in a movie are couples who come there together, for that express purpose. They are not each other's pickups. But how un-casual is fooling around in a public place like a movie theater? Especially if it is not just fooling around, as the term "one-night stand" implies? We still have not answered the question of what kind of lovemaking Weegee was after, in his picture.)

Plan of attack #2 continues Weegee's quest for heartfelt realism, though it necessarily involves a little disguise and deception (and accidentally, connotations of lost innocence). What happens is this: Weegee disguises himself as an ice cream vendor and moves among the ice cream eaters of the audience, though he is still after the couple making love. (The couple too busy to pay any attention to Weegee or his ice cream.) He doesn't say where he hid his camera, but it must have been close enough to whip out and shoot every time he saw something juicy. This time, he was closer to the action.

(It is an interesting though irrelevant sidelight that Weegee actually made a twenty-five percent commission on the ice cream he sold. Though he ate up all the profits.)

The editor of *Brief* was not satisfied. Oh, he got pictures of people sleeping, of people eating, of two people making love. But he was not satisfied. (So these particular two people, at least, could not really have been making love, as we now know it—as we now understand the term. Or else the editor would have been satisfied.) Weegee makes excuses. He admits the couple isn't being too "emotional" yet, because they're still "warming up." He's pretty sure they'll get warmer as the week goes on. The editor can't wait. He needs hotter pictures. How hot? How much warmer did Weegee expect that couple to get by the end of the week? How much warmer can they get, in a movie theater, even in an all-night 42nd Street theater?

A desperate Weegee resorts to subterfuge, manipulation, illusionism, sharing the profits. It was, after all,

35

a \$300 assignment. (No doubt in those days a lot of money.)

(Since I have had so little to recreate, facts-wise—and since the psychological motivation so far seems to be a clear-cut case of greed and ego, I might as well move beyond to the philosophical and moral implications behind the actions.)

Weegee goes out and gets a girl, a model, who owns a peekaboo dress, which makes her look enough like a "chippy" to fool people who judge girls by the way they look—or by the way they dress. Then he gets a guy from the Art Students League. (He probably figured that since art students have a reputation for doing anything for pleasure, a poor art student will do anything for pleasure and money. We don't know that Weegee's art student was poor, but most are. In any case, this one was getting paid.) Weegee takes the girl and the guy to a movie theater and tells them not to laugh, not to look at the camera, just make love. They do. (What do they do?) He gets the pictures soon enough, and they go home. Together.

(Some implications and speculations that come to mind: Can a voyeur create his own spectacle? Would that couple have met without Weegee, made love with greater or less enthusiasm without the camera watching and/or without Weegee paying? Does hiring models remind Weegee in any erotic way of hiring prostitutes, which he no longer does but may miss? Is it morally wrong to stereotype art students as poor? Why is the word "chippy" no longer used? Who would wear a peekaboo dress, even in 1951?)

Weegee prides himself on starting a romance, though he can't know, will never know, has never known if they continued to carry on, past that one-shot. But—suddenly, though without a climactic moment—I realize I know (I have known all along) what those two really did in the movie theater. Those were the days before *Playboy*, certainly before *Hustler*. *Brief* must have been pretty tame. It had to be, to get through the mails: those were the days of strict regulations about what could and could not get through the mails. So those pictures, even posed-to-order, could not have been that hot.

(All that was needed, after all, was a little knowledge of past federal postal regulations—a little historical perspective. However hot Weegee and his editor might have wanted those pictures, they were men of their time. As I am a woman of mine. And these days, morality is not in question. Though I cannot help being interested in what really happened, and why, with Weegee and his women.)

(1953)

It is 1953, the year of Natural Vision, and Weegee is well-experienced as a movie-theater voyeur.

(Does voyeurism require experience, or is it a natural talent? Only Natural Vision requires special glasses.)

The important thing to know is that in the picture taken at the Palace Theater during a 3-D movie, the only person who could have possibly seen Weegee taking her picture is the girl getting kissed, since she is not wearing glasses. Yet she is the least likely person to take notice of a crude and ugly middle-aged man like Weegee. She is in the heat of passion. Possibly more in the heat than her boyfriend, if that is what he is. He has not bothered to take off the glasses to get a look at what he's kissing. She's not that bad. Her face is the face of a nice girl, anyway. Her straight dark heavy brow is evidence of seriousness, as is

37

her straight dark heavy hair drawn back tightly from her forehead and temples in a virginal bun. And in the face of passion her eyes are demurely closed.

Possibly the boy's eyes are also closed behind his 3-D glasses. It is also possible that he is getting some kind of novel thrill by looking at his girlfriend through glasses that are supposed to block out everything but the screen. (Or is this only when one is looking directly at the screen, that everything peripheral is blocked out?) Of course, at that close range, he is only looking at a patch of skin on her face, most likely that sensitive large-pored area on the left side of her mouth. Most likely he is raising that sensitive area on the right side of her mouth into prickly hives by the prickly unshaved insensitive area on the left side of his mouth.

When you look at his girlfriend's body (assuming she is his girlfriend, and not just some casual pickup)—when you look at her body, you know—prickles around the mouth or not, pure brow or not—that she is in the heat of passion. She is too involved in what is happening, what is happening to *her*, to care that she looks like a chippy from the neck down. Not that they are really making love, as we now understand the term—only kissing, and embracing. But that boy's hand is slipped under her blouse at the shoulder. And her blouse is so gauzy, so see-through—a cheap nylon or rayon (if they have nylon and rayon back in 1953)—that we can even see her bra. (A white and strictly serviceable bra.) He hasn't got to the bra yet. His other hand is cupped just under her chin. Her feet are shamelessly bare. Her toes are curling under with ecstasy (unless the movie theater is cold and they are only shivering). Nobody's sitting next to her. (Except the boy.) The old bag on the other side of the boy is staring straight ahead at the screen we cannot see. In the photograph she is in darkness. Only the girl and the boy are illuminated by Weegee's invisible infrared flash. And as far as any of them are concerned—everyone wearing 3-D glasses and the girl who does not need to wear them to blind herself to everything but passion—as far as any of them are concerned, Weegee himself is as invisible as his flash, Weegee does not exist.

(Weegee is never in the picture. Weegee never does anything dramatic *in* the picture.)

Weegee's picture is so interesting, by itself, I have failed to consider Weegee at all. Or the scene from Weegee's point of view.

(Unless Weegee's point of view is my point of view, my point of view Weegee's, despite the years gone by between us.)

3. PORTRAIT OF THE PHOTOGRAPHER AS A CLAIRVOYANT

Throughout his career Weegee was known as a psychic.

(In the days before ESP was discovered to be scientifically measurable—if not explainable—being psychic was much more and much less than a special insight into or understanding of another's mind. It was rather a clairvoyance received from fate or a higher spiritual authority (God, ghosts) which allowed one, usually, to see ahead to the future. This most common and desired kind of clairvoyance is called precognition. This is what Weegee claimed to have.

There is also something called retrocognition, which as the name implies is knowledge of the past—knowledge of the past one would not ordinarily have. Retrocognition is not so ordinary, though desired. It is so rare that it is not even listed in Webster's *New Collegiate Dictionary*.)

Weegee prided himself on his psychic powers, though they were not really his own. He only received messages. Usually over his police radio.

(Weegee was not usually at a murder until after it happened. He always got the aftermath. He could only capture the past through the present.)

Could Weegee have gotten to a murder before it happened? During? During one of his famous-person lecture tours in the early fifties, upon arrival in each city he would announce that a murder would occur within twenty-four hours. Big cities being almost as dangerous then as they are now, the murder usually occurred. Once, in New Orleans, after the announcement was made, a reporter called Weegee with the news that the murder had just happened, just as predicted.

On that occasion, Weegee said no, that was not the murder he had foreseen. (A man shot his wife and then drowned himself in the Mississippi River, if it matters.) Did Weegee merely not like the details of that particular murder? Or was he beginning to worry that his predictions were nothing but self-fulfilling prophecies?

What if he had given up predictions and called them speculations? Would they still take on the authority of knowledge, could they somehow turn into truth? If not, would they compensate by being the product of his own imagination rather than messages from Fate?

(Who shoots Weegee's camera?)

40

(Who shot Weegee's camera?)

Weegee's egotism was mostly bluster. He lets it slip that he never stops considering himself lucky to get a woman. He admits that even after he is famous, he still has to pay them—with autographs, at least. And, humble man that he is, he himself is surprised when he makes a prediction in detail and every detail comes true.

(This is the magical part of the story, one that we don't have to understand, since even Weegee did not understand it.)

(Unless Weegee is lying, or lying by omission.)

In Washington, D.C. (where people know what happened long ago in history, though they are not sure about what is going on in their own day) a girl reporter—much too feisty for Weegee's taste—wants to know the future. She puts the psychic and his reputation on the spot. She and her editor want proof. She wants Weegee to predict what's going to happen that night (some unknown night in or around 1950). Pictures aren't enough for her. She wants written proof.

Now what Weegee does is drink (highballs), drink and concentrate. . . .

Then he has the inspiration. He doesn't tell us *how.* Except that he has it *suddenly,* as most inspirations come and go.

He writes out all the facts of his vision: a car thief, the cops in hot pursuit, the car crashing into a woman's dress shop, the inevitable capture—the time, the street—

It all happens, exactly. All the visible facts. All the drama of the instant. (None of the background. None of the past.) Weegee has surprised himself. He hopes he won't have to do it again, because he doesn't know how he did it.

But he's vindicated as a clairvoyant. (He's seen the future.) And he got some great pictures, some dramatic shots. (As it happened.) He's satisfied.

(We've looked at Natural Vision, chippies of the fifties, laws against pornography in the mails, the power of girlish passion.)

Though this was not what I was after.

The Real Life of Viviane Romance

IT WAS A VIOLENT NIGHT. It looked pretty enough, like fireworks. In fact there were fireworks in the sky. But before they were over a woman was dead.

I had a body on my hands already. In my arms actually. She was all doped up and cozy against me as I sat there on the beach watching the fireworks. They were pretty, like I said. Vivid reds and blues you don't usually see in the pastel California sky. But now it was dark, and the fireworks made the sky brilliant. I had earplugs in my ears. I didn't like the noise the explosions made, only the colors.

My gun is equipped with a silencer.

They were sisters, the corpse and the girl who couldn't keep herself awake. Twins. They were both languid types, usually from dope. Now the way you told one from the other was that the dead one was covered with blood.

She came crawling up to us and croaked. It took a minute before I realized that that meant she was dead.

I carried Ardith into the house and then came back for Vivian. She was either in shock or the dope hadn't worn off.

I did things to her she wouldn't remember the next day.

45

The next morning I had a rude shock. Vivian woke up, pointed a stubby unvarnished nail at me, and said, "You!"

It was then that I realized that it was not Vivian at all, but Ardith in my bed. Vivian was lying dead and unreported to the police in the parlor.

"You did it," Ardith continued accusingly.

But she couldn't pretend she hadn't liked it.

I considered my new situation. I had been in love with Vivian. But it had been Ardith in my arms the night before. The fireworks had diverted me from noticing any differences in smell, touch, speech patterns, etc. I am a visually oriented individual.

Ardith and I looked long at each other and then decided to kiss. This sealed our future intimacy. Now I could not suspect Ardith of the murder of her twin.

Business arrangements were concluded at breakfast. Vivian had been my client before, and my lover; now Ardith was to take her place as both. My duties were about the same. I had been hired to protect Vivian, but hadn't done such a good job of it. I was to do a better job with Ardith. This included keeping the police away. We also agreed to inspire each other.

We closed the door to the parlor and turned on the air-conditioning.

The neighbors noticed not a thing. Ardith paraded around the neighborhood, as Ardith during the day and Vivian at night. Everyone knew Vivian and I were lovers and they were used to the idea. Everyone was doing it.

I often found myself calling Ardith Vivian and she didn't seem to mind.

Vivian and Ardith were California girls of the kind I used to dream about. They both had long, flowing blonde hair, although Vivian's of course was now bloodstained.

Aside from this they were both colorless in the way

that health and sun seem to promote. Their skin was an even nut-brown shade that matched their leather thong sandals. Their lips were slicked with cocoa butter.

During the months I had been living with the twins their blonde hair had been progressively bleached out by the sun.

I was disappointed. To this disappointment I attribute my failure to adequately protect my client. We led a dull and colorless life. I had no way of knowing that one night there would be fireworks, just as I had no way of knowing that it was not my client watching them with me.

I had dreamed about a life of riotous color often enough when I lived in New York. I had had enough of those grey city streets. Times Square was pretty but noisy. Colored bars were really black and brown.

I envisioned quiet brilliant vistas in California and packed up my business cards.

First thing I did was throw the old business cards out and put my creative energies to work designing new ones. I wanted them printed up in hot pink, neon red, sapphire blue, chartreuse. But all the psychedelic printers had gone out of business. I had to settle for white ones. But under my name I printed, "Shamus," "Private Eye," "Private Operator," "Private Dick," or "Dick for Hire," variously.

It was a card of the last type that had brought Vivian Romance to my door.

Of course Vivian Romance was not her real name. It didn't matter. Not until she told me she was an actress. I told her that there was already an actress named Viviane Romance, or had been.

She hadn't heard of her. I explained that Viviane Romance had been a femme fatale of the French screen in the thirties and forties. I had always dreamed of seeing her in a film called *The White Slave*, but it never played anywhere. I did see her once, in a later movie called *Panique*, where she betrayed a stranger from the suburbs who loved her. I didn't tell Vivian that; I didn't want to give her any ideas. At least not that one. Instead I described Viviane in intimate physical detail. I described her innocent and yet oh-so-wise smile. Her fresh schoolgirl complexion refined to the heights of glamour by a discreet dusting of matte white powder. Her ruby-red lips. The slick shiny dress tightly encasing her hips and then slit from the top of her thighs to her knees. The huge blue and white polka-dot scarf tied in a bow at her neck, like a prize ribbon. The cigarette burning red-hot between her long slender red-varnished nails.

These details of clothing were obtained from an 8 × 10 black-and-white glossy I had had tacked up on my New York apartment wall. When lady clients visited me in my apartment I told them she was a missing person I was still searching for.

None of them ever took the hint. They took my remark literally and their performances in bed were, if inspired, not inspired by jealousy.

Ardith was jealous of my love for Vivian, though I was unaware of it at the time, and Vivian was jealous of my business, though she pretended to disdain it.

Vivian and I were not well suited. We misunderstood each other. She would say, during the calm following our violent passion:

"I can hardly stand this, what we do at night. I am so glad that during the day I am doped up enough that I can dream, peacefully."

Then she went on:

"I suppose you got into this business because you crave excitement."

I said:

"Not at all. This business of protecting you, for example, is quite dull. Not that I mind, as far as that goes. It just isn't very colorful."

48

"That's what I mean," she said. "You became a detective because you want an exciting and colorful life."

I told her that was just a cliché.

"That's all right," she said, perversely. "Those are difficult to avoid. What do you mean when you say you want color, if not excitement?"

"I mean I want color," I said. "Reds. Blues. You know."

Then she decided I was being sarcastic and no amount of truth I could tell her would convince her otherwise.

"Pass me the pipe," I said.

The above interchange was repeated on the average of four nights out of seven during the romance between Vivian and me, always ending with a puff of the pipe which made us forget the differences between us. If we were violent in our love during the remainder of the night we didn't know it or remember it the next day.

Now Vivian was dead and lying bloodstained in the parlor, and Ardith was acting strangely.

I figured it had to be fear of the police discovering the body and wondering why we hadn't done anything about it.

Both of us were doped up a lot these days. It was Ardith's idea. Parading around the neighborhood pretending to be Ardith or Vivian was straining her nerves. The only time she could relax at home was in the early evening, when she went out. She traveled to the drug haunts of Los Angeles, and brought back new tinctures for us to try.

Before, Ardith had done everything her twin had done, because they were twins. This was not vice versa because Vivian, being one minute older and an actress, had gained ascendancy in their sisterhood. So Vivian had called the shots, before she got shot.

Now, of course, with her body in the parlor, Vivian

belonged to the world of the past. Ardith and I tried to forget her predilections.

We concentrated instead on getting to know each other.

I discovered that Ardith was an artist. Or had been. Now, after a long dry spell, she was rediscovering her creativity. At any moment she was going to start spray-painting again.

I was happy that once again I had a girlfriend in the arts.

Ardith did not like being compared to her dead twin: Vivian had only been an actress and a not very successful one at that. Pretty girls like her were a dime a dozen in Hollywood. And anyway exhibitionism might be fun but it doesn't take much imagination.

Vivian, like most of her generation, had smoked dope. Her habits had been formed ten years ago and it never occurred to her to update them.

Ardith, on the other hand, though now a bit older than Vivian, quickly adopted a more modern outlook. She developed concepts that included the use of opium and laudanum, and drove down to the slums of Los Angeles to buy them.

Laudanum and opium did not prove to be readily available, so Ardith bought heroin and morphine and we pretended they were laudanum and opium.

It was becoming clear that Ardith intended to repudiate everything Vivian had stood for, and all in the name of Romance.

That was what Ardith was calling herself now. All she wanted of Vivian's was Romance—and me.

The new dope made for some colorful dreams, but when I woke up all I had to look at was Ardith's pasty face. She was so white you would have thought she was powdering her face with the stuff.

I found myself dreaming of a real red-blooded girl. So

one day I opened the door to the parlor and sneaked a look at Vivian's dead body.

Thanks to the air conditioner, Vivian was only a little bloated. One size bigger maybe. Her blood wasn't quite as red as it had been, but she had turned all sorts of pretty colors, mostly blue, purple, and green.

Whenever I got bored I would go and admire Vivian's body.

Naturally, Ardith caught on to what I was doing. She was a dope but she wasn't dumb. Or blind either. I was going to the parlor several times a day. Unnaturally, she was jealous of my interest in Vivian's body. She reminded me of the early days of our romance, when I used to call her Vivian. Whom did I really love, she asked me angrily.

I turned a deaf ear to her recriminations.

More dope was the obvious solution, but we decided to save opium for the romantic night. We were pinched for dough. I had long since spent Vivian's retainer and there was, obviously, no more money forthcoming from Vivian. Ardith was now my client but she was an aspiring artist and therefore poor. Vivian had left a will but nobody knew she was dead.

Not yet.

Any day they might start to wonder. Ardith was so jealous she would only leave the house to buy dope, and then it was so dark nobody in the neighborhood could see who she was supposed to be.

What might become the mystery of Vivian Romance's disappearance began to worry me, though the mystery of her murder was well in the past.

But old habits die hard. I was getting bored enough with our everyday life to give some thought to the murder. After all, the fireworks had been colorful.

If only I knew what had happened during those fireworks, I might have a clue as to how Vivian died. Maybe she hadn't been murdered after all. Maybe she had been hit by an exploding firecracker. Though that might not explain the blood.

I tried to discuss the possibilities with Ardith, but she refused to hear Vivian's name. I had to leave personalities out of the problem. I took a philosophical tack.

"Why were there fireworks, anyway?" I asked her. "It wasn't the Fourth of July."

Ardith replied that she hadn't heard any fireworks, but then she had been doped up.

That much I already knew.

As a matter of fact I had liked her better when she was all doped up. At least that night on the beach she had felt nice and cozy in my arms. The perfect companion to watch pretty fireworks in the sky with. Though at the time I had ascribed this perfection to her twin Vivian.

"So," Ardith countered, "you thought me perfect only when I had a twin, and when you didn't even know I was alive."

"No," I told her, "I thought you perfect when you didn't think to express yourself in this disgusting quarrelsome way, and I was too preoccupied with the fantastic colors in the sky to notice if you were one or the other of two identical clods of California earth."

It was quite a speech for a man of few words like me.

Ardith said irrelevantly:

"I'm going to change. And then if you don't notice me I just might disappear."

I told her that she was so white these days, it wouldn't surprise me if she did fade away.

Ardith thought I was joking. "I don't mean literally disappear, of course," she said coldly. "I mean disappear *for real*. Leave you. Then what would you tell the neighbors?"

"I'll tell them you were both sold into white slavery."

"White slavery has disappeared," Ardith informed me.

"So has opium," I reminded her.

"It just has another name these days," Ardith said thoughtfully. We stopped talking.

The next morning I had a rude shock. We'd used up all the dope and there was no more dough either.

I made plans for the present. During the day I was to work again as a public private detective and though she was my client Ardith would have to take care of herself.

She didn't need protection anymore anyway, she said. She was feeling very independent and modern.

In fact that afternoon she went by herself to a matinee showing of *The White Slave* starring Viviane Romance, and somebody mysteriously gave her a lot of money.

The best antique clothing stores in town were located near the drug-trafficking slums. Ardith began shopping at these stores before or after she bought our nightly ration of opium. She now dressed habitually in seamed stockings and clever veiled hats. "I look more like Viviane Romance than Vivian ever did," she boasted.

The neighbors naturally assumed both Ardith and Vivian were abandoning their former out-of-date clothes for more contemporary styles and did not think to look under the veil. Though naturally the face under the veil was the same. Plus white powder and red lipstick, of course.

Ardith's red lips were not for me. She only painted her face just before she went out. Besides clothes-shopping and drug-buying she was spending a lot of time at the movies. And she was quite secretive about what movies she'd seen. Whenever I asked she told me *The White Slave*.

"When are you going to really paint?" I asked Ardith the artist, fed up with the way she was spending so much money on clothes.

"When are you going to mind your own business?" Ardith snapped back.

53

Judy Lopatin

But by now I wasn't sure how to do it. I didn't have it in me to go out and find new clients. The detective business seemed at a dead end. I was never too good at detection anyway. Protection was my racket, but nobody seemed to want me to protect them. Much less dig into any mysteries of the past.

I decided not to look in the parlor anymore. It's still there. But after all this time it's not a pretty sight.

One night I dreamed that Ardith was a famous artist. I was jealous. She paraded around the city in her smart modern clothes and excited the admiration of every man in town. She betrayed me with each of these men, who were all the same to her anyway, nothing more than three-piece suits with lots of money. Then she betrayed me to the police. She told them I had killed Vivian. Suddenly, I saw fireworks. They were violet. And then Ardith came staggering along, spray-painted to death. All her pores were blocked but good.

Nuit Blanche

THE GIRL JILLY, just arrived in Paris, sat drinking a blue *sirop*, the specialty of the house. An ugly man, Carlos, had brought her to this bar, the Blue Room, a room that was not blue. It might be indigo, Jilly thought, that was not impossible: it was too dark in the place to see real colors. The Blue Room, if indigo, was not Indian in decor, though it was attached to an Indian restaurant upstairs, and a disco (not Indian) downstairs. It was the disco Carlos had promised her, for later, when the night began to have a life of its own. It was still well before midnight and already Jilly was beginning to feel sleepy. But according to the French horoscope magazine, *Astral*, tonight she was to have a *nuit blanche*. Jilly had guessed that a *nuit blanche* meant a night without sleep because the magazine had also predicted that she would be *épuisée* (exhausted) the next day.

A Hollywood Western was showing on the television screen above the bar, with the sound turned off completely. The Blue Room was too quiet for guns and horses. Jilly's friend Jean, a beatnik blonde, was listening to a youngish man with a receding hairline. Carlos had just disappeared. Jilly pretended to watch the movie with the others, four or five souls who seemed transfixed by the silent screen. None of them spoke to one another, as if they were strangers, or Blue Room-habitués of such long standing that there was nothing left to say. Though all of them had only nodded hello when she and Jean had been introduced, Jilly didn't think any of them were really mute, though one young woman was missing most of her teeth. Perhaps, like extras in a movie, they were paid to say nothing.

This is the Blue Room of Paris, Jilly told herself. It was hard to imagine life, French life, on the streets outside. She closed her eyes to picture it, and heard faint strains of Indian music she hadn't noticed before; or had the music just begun? And there was another sound, a rustle, like a spangled costume hitting the floor. She opened her eyes again to see what was happening. The *patronne* was not stripping, or even dancing, but merely swaying her large body (clad in raw Indian silk) heavily against the black lacquered bar. Jilly imagined that under certain circumstances, perhaps a different upbringing or too much blue liqueur, the creepiness she felt in the Blue Room could seem mystical, even magical. It wasn't really the music, it was the Queen: the Queen did not seem quite real.

Of course the *patronne*, like all ordinary Frenchwomen, had a real name—Carlos had introduced her as Mademoiselle Somebody, though behind her back he referred to her as *La Dame*, as if she were the only one in the world. But before Jilly had had time to worry what to call her, Jean had whispered, "She looks like The Queen." It sounded perfect. A queen like Cleopatra, perhaps, though Egypt and India were not the same places at all—but here in the Blue Room, Jilly felt, national boundaries were blurred. She was sure the blue *sirop* came from the Caribbean, the *West* Indies. And there was no reason why an Indian bar/restaurant/nightclub in Paris should have an English name, except that the Queen spoke English perfectly, in a hushed, articulate whisper. "Late Elizabeth Taylor," Jilly whispered back to Jean. Their whispers were real ones, lower than the Queen's. The Queen's voice was so peculiar there seemed to be no word in the English language to describe it. It was high-pitched, girlish but insinuating—nothing like Liz Taylor's now. But her eyes were painted in dark black lines and contours, just like Cleopatra's in the movies or a prostitute's in real life. No, Jilly amended, not a prostitute, the Queen was too old and big for that: a madam, maybe.

Suddenly Jilly felt the Queen's eyes on her. The Queen wanted to say something to her, draw her out, enmesh her in something foreign—a conversation she wouldn't understand because it was foreign, French. The Queen said, "Would you like some more blue liqueur?" She said it softly and precisely, but in English. Jilly nodded. She should have felt reassured that the Queen merely wanted to practice her English with her, but still she felt uneasy about the Queen's diction, her pauses and painted eyes. Even though Jilly's eyes, too, were painted in black lines. But there was nothing else to do but talk to the Queen, or at least listen to her. It was impossible to get in on the intimate chat Jean was having with the balding young man, who seemed to have a romantic nature even if he was too cool to become instantly smitten—he was telling Jean, in quiet, measured tones, something about how he was looking for a *mariage blanc,* he hoped with an American. Jilly drank some more of the blue *sirop* even though she knew it was bad for a *nuit blanche;* she would never stay awake if she got drunk. Was there an essence of a *nuit blanche,* she wondered, or did it just go on and on until morning? The essence of Nuit Blanche . . . it sounded like a perfume. Except that no such perfume existed. She was, however, wearing Shalimar, very French and at the same time Eastern for the occasion. Mysterious and Parisian. Jilly sniffed her wrist and wished that Carlos would reappear: he gave her the creeps but he was easy to talk to.

Carlos spoke French slowly and precisely, probably because he wasn't really French. His first name was Spanish and his last name sounded Italian, so he could have been anything.

Jilly had only met Carlos earlier that same day, but it seemed like ages ago. It seemed the day had already ended long ago, at dusk, when a woman on the street had pressed upon her a bunch of orange flowers only slightly wilted, just because she hadn't wanted them anymore. Jilly thought how lucky it was that the flowers were orange because they matched the hotel room wallpaper, which Jean thought ugly but Jilly didn't mind. As soon as the woman left her with the flowers Carlos extracted from her a promise to meet him later that night. She could hardly wait until he left, too, and then she rushed home to their Latin Quarter hotel to tell Jean the good news, not even waiting for Jean to come out of the W.C. across the hall to tell her that maybe both of them could get jobs as extras in the French film industry.

Yes, Jilly had to admit to herself, that was the only reason she'd accepted Carlos's evening invitation: he was ugly but he was in the movies. Though her motives had been purer when he had first approached her. He was somebody to talk French with.

Talking French, that was what Jilly was in Paris for, besides getting a job, so she could stay longer in Paris and talk French more. But she had started her day alone, sitting in the Luxembourg Gardens and writing in English in her journal. She found it hard to say much of anything because nothing much so far had happened. She knew she was to meet Jean later in the famous Select Bar in Montparnasse but she had no way of knowing that Jean wouldn't make it and that Carlos would appear instead. So when an odd young Frenchman approached her in the Luxembourg Gardens she might have put down her notebook to talk to him, and she did. But after she replied that no, she was not an *étudiante*, she told him to go away. His blue eyes were too bright; he looked like a maniac.

"Pourquoi?" he asked her. Maybe he was just an idiot: he had a silly grin, and after Jilly had said *"Parce que"* and pointed to her notebook, he kept asking her *pourquoi* over and over again, stupidly. Jilly wanted him to go away but since he was a colorful character as well as a stupid one she felt a bit guilty. In her notebook she had just remarked that in Paris, everything and nothing seemed possible at the same time, and that after all there was nothing very adventurous about sitting in a park or café waiting for adventure. In fact, she hadn't even finished that last sentence when the park Romeo (she'd already forgotten his name) had interrupted with his curiosity about whether or not she was a student. Jilly figured it might have been better if she'd said yes, because to the world, to men, in Paris, girls with notebooks are either students or romantics, and romantics are the easiest in the world to fool. Jilly didn't think she was a fool, but this young man certainly was, and it wasn't until Jilly let her voice become dark and threatening that the park Romeo finally left her. She opened her notebook, finished her thought, and then added with a pang of guilt that after all there are no adventures but *les rencontres, n'est-ce pas?*

Nobody in Paris says *n'est-ce pas* any more, Jilly then reflected hopelessly, as she walked through the Luxembourg Gardens to the Select.

The Queen poured some more of the blue *sirop* into Jilly's glass, this time without asking, and smiled a secret smile. Jilly said *"Merci"* automatically, hoping that the specialty of the house would also be on the house: she had to watch her money too carefully to pay for expensive drinks. She would have preferred a rum and Coke, but cocktails in Paris were the most expensive of all, and Jilly wasn't sure if she was Carlos's guest when Carlos was not around. Unless she had suddenly become the Queen's guest. It did seem that, for some reason, the Queen was quite charmed by Jilly, though she knew Jilly was just a poor girl in Paris: Jilly had confessed that she'd just been in Paris six days and needed to get a job fast. Then through the haze of blue liqueur she remembered to add, "But that may be impossible, because it's against the law for Americans to work in Paris, unless they are married to somebody French." Anyone, after all, might be hand in glove with the police. The Queen laughed. "But it isn't impossible," the Queen said, as if the Blue Room were not governed by French law, or were not really in Paris at all. At least not the Paris of the police. "What would you like to do?" "Teach English," Jilly said, "or anything."

The Queen looked like she was going to say something else, but suddenly a new rhythm began playing on the sound system, another Indian tape, but janglier. The Queen's Liz eyes caught the velvety brown ones of the young boy who was playing bartender. "Turn this up," she commanded him in English, "this is Classic."

A chill ran down Jilly, so extraordinarily had the Queen pronounced the word *classic*. At the same time she wondered what nationality the young bartender might be. She imagined teaching him English, whatever the Queen hadn't already taught him. The Queen fixed her eyes on Jilly again. "You speak English very well," Jilly ventured.

The Queen's eyes shut slightly, intensifying the enigmatic effect painted on by her eye makeup. "Of course."

Jilly felt vaguely disappointed. "You've lived in England or America then?"

"Oh yes. I lived in New York City for quite a few months, years ago. . . . I wanted to start a theatre there. It was to do only the works of Molière. It would have been wonderful."

"But you never did?" Jilly could not help asking. She did not know enough about Molière to ask anything else: Molière was French. It didn't seem like a likely passion for the Queen, except that Molière was also Classic.

"No, it never happened." The Queen's lips curled into a fixed smile.

"*Où est-ce que vous habitiez à New York?*" Jilly asked quickly.

"Central Park West. A lovely apartment," the Queen pronounced. Jilly nodded. She could imagine it, large and sunny, with a blue room perhaps, sometime in the foreign New York of twenty years ago, when the Queen was young. "But do not think I learned English in New York," the Queen added suddenly. "I merely improved my accent. I learned English as a child, from books. I read many, many books in English, aloud, one after the other."

"*Ah oui?*" Jilly said politely. Then she remembered that that expression might not be really correct, so she said, "*Ah bon?*"

"Yes," the Queen said, "I devoured them."

The Queen's eyes were glittering. Jilly thought she looked triumphant, or maybe just happy, as if she were no longer revealing secrets but simply telling a favorite story. "I performed for all my father's friends. He brought me many, many books in English. He told me, nothing is impossible to understand. Just keep reading. I read every book aloud, every word even if I didn't know what I was saying. It was magical, soon I knew everything. Just hearing the words . . . my voice pronouncing strange words . . . it was magical. Yes, and my father thought so, too. When his friends came over for dinner at our house, he would introduce me, I would come out with my latest book and perform."

"Act out the story?" Jilly asked.

"No, I simply read them aloud. They were magical, impossible to act out," said the Queen. Jilly wondered what the English books might have been. Were they fairy tales? Had the books been magical, or only the sound of the Queen's voice pronouncing words she didn't understand?

Jilly thought of the *roman policier* she had carried with her to Paris, bought at a French bookstore in New York. A Simenon. It was so impossible to understand she had abandoned it, temporarily. "I am reading a mystery in French," she told the Queen, "to myself."

"Oh, but it must be aloud," the Queen insisted. "That is the trick. Read aloud to yourself, although of course having a public is even better." She paused. "New York still needs a theatre doing only Molière, but so much time has passed without it happening. . . ."

And then Carlos reappeared.

Carlos had a way of appearing, Jilly thought, when you weren't expecting him, or anything like him, but hoping for something to happen. He was like an ugly gnome who seemed at first repulsive, but then turned into a kind of Prince Charming. No, gnome wasn't the right metaphor, Jilly thought, he must be a frog, even though he wasn't really French. Anyway, if a girl was brave enough to look past his ugliness for the sake of speaking French, and she was smart enough not to believe everything she thought she understood, then anything might happen.

In the Select Bar that afternoon, mid-afternoon, were only a handful of customers—all of them what the French call "marginals": beatniks and hippies, political revolutionaries and prostitutes, ordinary criminals. Most of the *marginals* in the Select that afternoon seemed to be hippies. Although favorably disposed to *marginals*, Jilly, marginally a beatnik type herself, had a modern scorn for hippies, particularly when they were in Paris, where they didn't seem to belong. Most of the *marginals* in the Select looked as though they made their living singing old folk songs in the Place St.-André-des-Arts—a hard life that must be, Jilly thought, when a cup of coffee at a decent café costs eight francs.

After the *café crème* she'd ordered arrived, Jilly took out her notebook and glanced at what she had written in the six days she had been in Paris. Her experiences, what there were of them, were exhausted, and she had exhausted her imagination, *epuisée,* just as the horoscope magazine had predicted (only she wasn't supposed to be exhausted until tomorrow, after the *nuit blanche* tonight). Jilly put the notebook away and took out an assorted collection of postcards, mostly cheap views of the Eiffel Tower and more expensive prints of posters from the Belle Epoque. What a shame it was, Jilly thought, that the Belle Epoque no longer lived in Paris, except for some seedy shops selling black lingerie in Pigalle. She remembered that the black lingerie had been very imaginative, more exotic than any she'd seen in New York, probably because it was Parisian. She wondered if men all over the world found black lingerie from Paris exciting.

In the end Jilly chose the odd postcard of the lot, a very modern picture of a punkish-but-Parisian woman who slightly resembled her, sitting on a motorcycle and wearing cheap red plastic sunglasses, a black leather jacket. It looked to Jilly as if the woman owned an extra set of breasts, but then she realized they must only be ribs. "Here I am in Paris, home of the Science of Beauty," Jilly wrote on the postcard to a New York friend. She wondered what to say next, and looked up for inspiration. An ugly little man with a long medieval beard was stooping before her: Carlos.

"You are just passing the time?" Carlos asked her in French, motioning to her writing.

"*Oui, oui,*" Jilly replied. Unlike Jean she did not think of postcards as sending off pieces of Paris. That was silly, even sillier than writing in a notebook, which was actually important, even if the park Romeo hadn't realized it. But since writing postcards was a tourist's occupation it was natural that Carlos did not dream he was interrupting anything important, even though he himself was a kind of writer.

Yes, he'd told her all about himself very quickly, that he wrote the scripts of movies, even before she'd told him about the job she was hoping to get in Paris, teaching English or typing up some American professor's notes or (it was not so impossible, a friend of hers had done it) becoming an extra, a *figuerant*, in a French movie.

"Perhaps I can help you," Carlos then said.

Jilly felt strange. Perhaps he didn't really believe she wanted to be an extra, had seriously considered the idea before meeting him, a man in the movies who might help her. It was just a stroke of luck, fate, coincidence. Or was it? Perhaps Carlos was only pretending to be in the movies: that role was classic. "Have you written any movies I know?" she asked him in French.

Carlos mentioned a very famous film, a political docudrama of some twelve years ago. Jilly had heard of the film but not of Carlos. She wondered if a book somewhere in Paris might list the film and its writer. It might not be a French film; it took place in Greece, and since in America the subtitles had been in English she couldn't really remember what language the actors had spoken.

"French," Carlos informed her, "it was a French movie. Some of the actors were French, you know, the famous ones, others were Greek. But they dubbed their voices from Greek into French. It's very common, dubbing the voices of foreigners."

It took Jilly a few moments to understand what he was talking about, that *doubler* meant "to dub," and then she thought she understood too well what he meant, because he said next:

"I will check the notices in *Le Film Francais*, to see if any of my friends are making movies soon. Maybe they could use you."

"*Comme un figuerant?*" Jilly said.

66

"Yes, or who knows, maybe a larger part. Yes, why not?"

"I'm not an actress," Jilly replied warily. "Aren't there enough—too many—French actresses already?"

Perhaps her French was so bad he did not understand her, for Carlos only smiled and repeated, "We use foreigners all the time, in the movies. It is quite easy to dub in the voices."

"This is just like a scene from a bad movie," Jilly said, as if it were a joke he was in on. Then she realized she had spoken in English. *"Tu sais, la fille très innocente, ses rêves, le cinéma . . . elle fait la connaissance d'un homme qui dit . . . qui lui dit . . . l'avenir dans le cinéma."* They both laughed then, and she added in as nice a way as possible, but in her best French accent so he would understand her, that she was too smart for all that. All she wanted with Carlos was friendship, platonic.

"Yes, yes, *c'est bien,*" Carlos agreed quickly. His hands closed over hers across the table, to seal the agreement.

Jilly could hardly remember the rest of the conversation; it was almost as if she were drunk, even though she'd just been drinking coffee, there at the table with Carlos. An hour must have passed, maybe more, and then suddenly the bar filled with businessmen just released from their offices, plus a few *marginals* Carlos recognized as his friends from the film industry. He brought Jilly up to the bar, with his arm around her protectively, and introduced her to a short slovenly man who was a film director, and some others, cameramen mostly. Soon they had seated Jilly on a bar stool, in the midst of them, and arranged for a rum and Coke to be delivered in front of her. She could not understand anything they were saying. It was all too fast, and she was too tired to listen hard enough. Carlos had worn her out. Jilly began to feel a little scared, imagining what they might be saying about her, but then she reminded herself that she was perfectly

67

safe in the bar and that what she didn't know couldn't hurt her.

But how, Jilly wondered, did they expect to seduce her with a torrent of French she couldn't understand? Because the businessmen did seem to want to seduce her. The movie-marginals had found her too stupid, even Carlos had drifted away, and now she was left with two businessmen, one handsome white-haired man in his fifties and a much younger and handsomer sharp French wolf named Yvon. The man in his fifties, being old enough to be her father, might have amused Jilly if she hadn't found him so confusing: he was either trying to give her his phone number, or trying to get hers. He also warned her (Jilly thought) that she should not be wasting her time with Carlos, who was a foreigner and a low sort, everyone thought so. Jilly knew he was very drunk, but she wondered if he was right, if Carlos was dangerous. Or did he only mean that Carlos was too ugly for her to waste her time on?

The younger businessman, Yvon, had long laughing teeth, brilliantined hair, a very suave manner. He could have been an actor, Jilly thought. "She's charming, isn't she charming?" Yvon asked the drunk man in his fifties. Yvon kept grabbing Jilly's arm and trying to pull her somewhere, and Jilly kept removing his hand from her arm, but not without some regret; she remembered it perfectly. After many minutes of what seemed to be extravagant compliments or indecent proposals in rapid-fire French, Jilly made out that Yvon was asking her to go for a cup of coffee with him. He was very insistent. Jilly looked around for Carlos, but he was nowhere in sight. "*Je ne peux pas, merci,*" she told Yvon, trying to sound flirtatious but firm. Yvon just laughed and kept grabbing her arm and repeating his offer, coffee, now, let's go.

"Go home," someone whispered in English in her ear. It was Carlos, reappeared out of nowhere, Jilly thought, or maybe the W.C. "This is not for you, this bar." He insisted on ushering her out of the bar and walking her part of the way home. "I'll meet you outside," Jilly told him. For some reason she did not want to be seen leaving the bar with Carlos, even though they did have a date later that night for the Blue Room: "a disco I go to all the time," Carlos had said, "I am dear friends with the *patronne.*" Jilly had never heard of the place, but it was a night-spot, so there was a chance the Blue Room might provide a memorable *nuit blanche.* She wondered if there would be other Yvons at the Blue Room, handsome wolves who would keep her up all night, and if she would lose her chance to be in the movies if she succumbed to their charms. Maybe it was just this wolf Carlos disapproved of. Jilly said goodbye to Yvon, jerked her arm away from him one last time, and hurried out the door to meet Carlos on the street.

Carlos was still waiting, but he looked dark. They walked down the street in silence. Then Jilly said, "What is it with Yvon, why don't you like him?" "Because I know him," Carlos said. "He would have kept after you until you had gone to bed with him." "But I wouldn't have let him," Jilly said quickly.

Carlos smiled. "You would have had no choice. He can be violent." "*Vraiment?*" Jilly said disbelievingly. "Oh yes," Carlos said. "He's notorious at the Select. He always gets what he wants." Yes, Jilly thought, he was jealous. She tried to remember the businessman's warning about Carlos: what exactly had he said?

As they neared the corner of the Boulevard Montparnasse and the Boulevard St. Michel, Jilly was just about to say goodbye to Carlos when the woman with the wilted orange flowers rushed at her. Jilly shrunk back, not understanding, afraid she was being asked to buy them. Carlos told her, "She wants to give them away, they're free," took the flowers from the woman and gave them to Jilly. "That was very nice of her," Jilly said with relief. "Oh, but she didn't want them anymore," said Carlos. "Don't forget about tonight. The Blue Room."

Jean, whom Jilly had taken along this evening for protection, was looking sleepy as the youngish balding man in the Blue Room bar was talking to her. Jilly knew Jean was not really sleepy, just bored, though she told Carlos that it was just that Jean wasn't wearing her contact lenses and so she could hardly see anything, and that made her very tired and bored-looking. Carlos seemed intrigued by Jean's blindness. Well, Jilly thought, there must be room for two American girls in the movies, especially two girls with different haircolors. Not everyone preferred blondes. She wondered if Carlos and his dear friend the Queen (a brunette) had ever been lovers. It was not impossible. They were both middle-aged; Carlos had once been famous, and the Queen, however fat and cheap she looked now, might once have been beautiful.

"Would you like to see my restaurant?" the Queen asked Jilly in her insinuating voice. Jean was summoned away from the bald man and the Queen appointed Carlos to escort them on the tour. He led them up several flights of stairs and down another, until they found themselves in a large room that was the Indian restaurant. Jilly felt that a mystery had been solved: the room was decorated in blue, ordinary blue. The tablecloths, though, were white. Only two of the tables were occupied by diners. "Nobody's here," Jean whispered to Jilly, "what's wrong with this place?" There was only one waiter, who had nothing to do. He was a young boy with buck teeth who seemed genuinely Indian and spoke English, though not as well as the Queen. He wanted to know where Jean and Jilly were from. "New York? I have a cousin there. I also saw a movie about New York today," he told them, smiling widely. Jilly thought the poor young woman in the bar could use some of the waiter's teeth. "The movie was good but it was about homosexuals and I don't like that," the waiter went on. "I like sexual but not homosexual." Jilly wondered what opportunities for either sex the waiter might have. He did look happy. Maybe he was just happy to be working in the Blue Room.

The tour of the restaurant was concluded in a matter of minutes. After descending only one short flight of stairs, Jilly and Jean found themselves back in the small Blue Room bar. Jilly hurriedly told the Queen that the restaurant was lovely. "Would you like to try my cuisine?" asked the Queen. Jilly was not sure whether or not the meal would be on the house, and besides, after she had returned from the Select she and Jean had had a nice meal of bread, wine, and cheese in their hotel room. Cheap and French at the same time. "Thank you, but we ate already, we're not really hungry," Jilly said. The Queen looked annoyed. Jilly felt she could not bear to sit in the bar a moment longer. She turned to Carlos and said, "Is it late enough to go down to the disco?" "Yes, if you want to," Carlos said reluctantly, as if he had forgotten the purpose of visiting the Blue Room.

The disco was deserted. Not exactly, Jilly amended to herself, there were a few couples dancing. They looked very young, teenagers. She could not imagine Carlos coming to the disco regularly to dance or even drink. He belonged more to the peculiar strained atmosphere of the Blue Room, the bar that is, except he hadn't stayed there long. Where had he been all that time? Jilly wondered. For some reason his absence made her even more uneasy than his presence. The restaurant or the disco, those were the only places he could have been, unless there was a secret room somewhere else on the premises, a room even bluer than the restaurant and not as ordinary. But probably Carlos had only been eating his dinner, alone. Jilly had just settled on this conclusion when Jean whispered, "This place looks like a set-up for white slavery." This remark seemed to Jilly to come out of the blue and she was astonished. The young people dancing looked normal enough, though not numerous. "What gives you that idea?" she asked Jean, thinking maybe it had been some information or hint from the bald young man.

"Nobody's here," Jean said. "What about all those young kids dancing?" Jilly pointed out. "They don't look natural," Jean said. "They're lures." "They look like high-school kids to me. *Lycée* kids," Jilly said. "They don't look normal to you because we don't look normal. White slavery, what a ridiculous idea. Nobody is a white slaver any more." But as soon as she said that she could see the whole scene quite clearly, white slavery in the Blue Room, with the Queen as madam-kidnapper. It sounded like a movie, or a joke: it was something to write about on a postcard, Jilly decided, like black-lingerie shops, a dark side of Paris that might or might not exist.

Carlos, smiling, insisted on ordering both Jean and Jilly new drinks. He didn't ask them what they wanted, so Jilly got another blue *sirop* and Jean got the same, her first. "It's horrible," Jean whispered to Jilly. "Sickly-sweet." Jilly agreed, thinking it was funny she hadn't noticed this before. "Maybe it's drugged," she joked to Jean. But she was not feeling sleepy anymore. Maybe it was the music, those pounding rhythms—even though she didn't like disco she had to admit it was hypnotic, in a different way from Indian music. It kept you tapping your foot. "I'm going to take a look at the place," she told Carlos, leaving him to Jean and her blind attention.

Near the dancers were some cushions, and a couple sitting on them—almost swallowed up, Jilly thought. They looked as though they were about to start kissing at any moment. She took a few steps away from them and watched the dancers for a few seconds. They still looked teenage, not just the girls but the boys too. In fact they were so normal-looking they gave her the creeps. She shuddered, remembering the way the Queen had pronounced the word *classic,* and suddenly felt that she and Jean did not belong in Paris. Maybe it was because they were beatniks, modern-day but not Parisian. Carlos, though, seemed to like her type. She decided she had nothing else to do but go back to him.

Then she spotted the balding young man sitting at the other end of the disco bar, Jean's balding young man. But Jean was now talking with Carlos. Jilly passed them by without looking their way and sat casually next to the young man.

"Tell me about yourself," the young man said to Jilly, as if he were expecting her.

"I live in New York," Jilly said. It was the first thing that came into her head. "Do you like Molière?"

"Molière? Not much," the young man smirked. "That's a strange thing for an American girl to say," he added after a pause.

"*La Dame* is very interested in Molière," Jilly explained. "She wanted to open a Molière theatre in New York. That's why I mentioned it."

"Yes, and when one thinks of New York, one thinks of Molière theatres," the man grinned. Jilly thought that despite his receding hairline he seemed very arrogant, very Parisian.

"Actually Molière theatres don't exist," Jilly said. It was meant to be a rebuke, but the young man was grinning even more arrogantly. Jilly nodded in the direction of Jean. "We think *La Dame* looks exactly like the madam of a white slavery establishment." As soon as she said it, the young man's face darkened. "Isn't it," she continued, trying to strike a lighter tone, "isn't this a strange place?"

"That was an incredible thing to say, horrible," the young man said.

73

"It was just a joke," Jilly said.

"No," the young man said, "you meant it." His face was still dark, sullen.

"No, my friend thought so, I said it was impossible," Jilly said. She didn't know what else she could say. "You are a good friend of *La Dame?*"

"No," said the young man surprisingly, "I don't like it here. I only come to play chess."

"You're not playing chess now," Jilly said, meanly she hoped.

But the young man seemed relaxed now. "And what do you know about white slavery?"

"Nothing," Jilly said.

"Exactly. It is only a scenario in the cinema. It exists no more in real life."

"Prostitution does," Jilly said feebly.

"Yes, prostitution, but prostitutes want to be prostitutes. *Comprends?*" said the young man.

"*Oui*," Jilly responded automatically. She wanted to agree, to say that no desires were immoral if they were actually voiced, but she didn't know the words in French to say it. Then she asked herself if prostitutes really wanted to be prostitutes. They might just be girls who ran out of cash too soon. It could happen to anyone. Jilly had not told the Queen, or Carlos, but she had been in Paris before—a year ago, for just two weeks. An acquaintance in New York, a middle-aged writer, had told her to look someone up, an American woman he had known from his college days. She had lived in Paris for years now and, he thought, she was working as a prostitute. Jilly had been afraid to telephone her until the very last day of the two weeks, when it was too late to arrange a meeting. She was afraid she had already seen the woman: one night in Pigalle, near the Place Blanche, Jilly had looked into a doorway and seen black fishnet stockings, black leather shorts, a black leather jacket. It could have been any prostitute and yet Jilly had this odd sense that she had caught a glimpse of the woman she was looking for.

When she finally telephoned the writer's friend (after drinking some wine), the woman told Jilly she was very busy working, translating business letters mostly, but that she had also just recorded some disco songs under a different name. "Truth is stranger than fiction," the woman had said.

"What do you do, to live?" Jilly asked the young man.

"I'm a writer," he said. She was not surprised. She asked his name but of course she had never heard of it. "What do you write?" she asked then.

"*Romans policiers,*" said Gérard. "I also like to read them. Not Molière." He smiled.

"Yes, I like *romans policiers* too," Jilly agreed. Finally they could find each other *sympathique.* "I am reading one now which begins with a woman *qui fait l'auto-stop.*"

"Yes," said Gérard. "Many *romans policiers* start in such a fashion. *Faire l'autostop,* it's very dangerous. All sorts of adventures can happen."

"I also have a Simenon," Jilly said. "I can't understand it. It's not a very famous Simenon. Nobody has translated it into English. Have you read *The Blue Room?*"

"*Comment?*" Gérard said.

"I just remembered, it's a novel by Simenon," Jilly said. "I read it in New York, in English. It's not the one I brought with me to Paris."

"No, that would be too much of a coincidence," Gérard said.

"Oh, but I believe in coincidences," Jilly said. "Do you believe in astrology?"

"Of course," Gérard said. "My mother is an astrologer, also a *clairvoyante.*"

"*Vraiment?*" Jilly said excitedly. "Does she have an ad in the horoscope magazines?"

75

"Yes, I believe so. Most of the time," Gérard said. "Her name is Denise."

"I'll look for it," Jilly said. "Is it Denise, or Madame Denise?"

"Madame Denise, naturally," Gérard said. He was annoyed again. "She is my mother, she is married."

"I only thought . . ." Jilly began. She could not explain that she was only wondering if Denise was called Madame like most of the other clairvoyants who advertised in the magazine, to make them sound more exotic. Or maybe just as a convention. She thought that probably Gérard was a conventional romantic sort; he was looking for a *mariage blanc. Blanc* in this case, she supposed, meant pure. She said, "My horoscope said tonight I would have a *nuit blanche.*"

"Ah," said Gérard, "that is not so pleasant."

"*Une nuit blanche*—does this mean a night without sleep?"

"*Oui,*" he agreed.

"Yes, I thought so. But I also thought it might mean a night without dreams," Jilly said. "When you don't dream you are very tired the next day, because you don't have the right kind of sleep, and my horoscope said the next day I would be *très épousée.*"

Gérard smiled. "*Épuisée,* you mean."

"Yes, *épuisée,* what did I say?"

"You said *épousée*—married. An understandable error," Gérard said. "Why are you in Paris?"

"I don't know," said Jilly.

"Are you a tourist? A student?"

"No," Jilly said. "I'm just living in Paris. I want to get a job," she added.

"And how long do you wish to stay in Paris?"

"A few months. Longer if I can make some money," Jilly said.

Gérard leaned toward her. "Do you want to marry a Frenchman?"

"Anything is possible," said Jilly lightly.

"Yes, nothing is impossible, when you have enough money," Gérard said. "My *romans policiers* are very successful. Not as successful as Simenon, but who cares? I make a good living. I have enough money to go to New York."

"Oh, do you want to go to New York?"

"Yes, but first I must meet an American girl who is willing to marry me. Then I can go to New York and stay there, and she—she can stay in beautiful Paris." He was smirking.

"Yes, Paris is very beautiful," Jilly agreed. "But you and I, we could not really do such a thing. I heard you say to my friend Jean that you wanted something beautiful, a *mariage blanc.*"

"Yes, yes," Gérard said impatiently, "that's just what I am proposing, a *mariage blanc.*"

Suddenly Jilly understood everything. She felt defeated, even though she had never had any desire to marry balding Gérard. She said, "I am sure that there are many girls in New York who might want to come to Paris, who would marry you."

"Yes, but there are many girls already in Paris, without any means to stay here—who have come on a whim and don't want to leave. Like Jean, perhaps, or you," Gérard said.

"I don't know about Jean," Jilly began.

"She took my name and address for the future. And you?"

"I could never marry for money," Jilly said.

"But there's no other reason to marry," Gérard said angrily. "What is it, do you still believe in *Prince Charmant?*"

It was such a coincidence, Gérard mentioning Prince Charming, when earlier that evening she had been thinking of Carlos that way, not Carlos himself exactly but his promises. And now Carlos was charming Jean in the same way. "No," Jilly said.

"I don't believe you. You do still believe," Gérard said. "But all that is not reality."

"You believe in the stars," Jilly said defensively.

"That's different."

"No it's not," Jilly said. "If you believe in fate you can believe in Prince Charming."

Gérard smiled, a very calm smile. "But fate is not so pleasant. Do you think it is? Are you stupid?"

Suddenly the Queen appeared. "When you're ready," she told Jilly, "come see me."

It was still before midnight, but Jilly wanted to leave the Blue Room. Jean was only too glad to leave the company of Carlos: beards such as his made her sick, she told Jilly. Jilly said that wasn't fair but she understood. She told Carlos, even though it wasn't true, that they wanted to leave because they were very sleepy. She didn't want to hurt his feelings. He no longer seemed potentially dangerous, not nearly as dangerous as Gérard; he was just a middle-aged has-been. But the Queen—the prospect of going up to the bar to see the Queen made Jilly uneasy. She wondered if the Queen was going to accuse her of something—of being stupid maybe. Or had Gérard somehow conveyed the message that Jilly thought the Queen a white slaver?

But the Queen was all smiles. "Was that man bothering you?" she asked Jilly. "He's a bit peculiar." "No, not really," Jilly said. "I didn't want him to bother you," the Queen said. "There's no reason why you should bother with him. Will you come tomorrow to sample my Indian cuisine? You and your friend, both of you." "Well, I'm no expert on Indian cuisine," Jilly said. The Queen stopped smiling. "You don't want to taste my cuisine? But it's very good, very savory." "Yes, of course," Jilly said, feeling trapped. "I

78

just meant I didn't know enough about it." The Queen
looked satisfied. She smiled her secret smile and leaned
forward confidentially, whispering in Jilly's ear. "Maybe I
will hear of a job for you. I don't know, something to make
you some money . . . maybe you could leave your name and
address, your telephone number too." Jilly nodded; she
could not resist. "And you will come to dinner tomorrow
night?" the Queen added. "Yes," Jilly said, and then she
was out the door, on the street.

Carlos walked them to the *métro* and said goodbye.
"You'll find me at the Select almost every afternoon," he
told Jilly. "Give me a week or so to talk to my friends."
Jilly thanked him, but she no longer believed him, or his
life in the movies. She was thinking about a nearer future,
what might happen the next night if she returned to the
Blue Room as the Queen's guest, eating the Queen's food
and learning her tricks, her magic words.

"Une nuit blanche," Jilly whispered to herself, barely
aloud, in her bed. Jean was already asleep. Jilly wished she
could fall asleep, too, to dream of white slavery, black
leather, blue movies. And savory Indian dinners. She
thought that if she dreamed at all, it might be only about
a free meal.

It was only just past midnight. The prediction of the
horoscope magazine had not come true. There were hours
to go before morning, she would certainly fall asleep
sometime during the night. She had not spent a *nuit
blanche*, not even one long night, so why did she feel as if
she had spent weeks and weeks in Paris, weeks without
end? And yet Jilly knew there would be an end, weeks or
months ahead, when her money ran out. But by then it
might seem like years. Paris would go on and on, many
nights like this. She would probably never get in the
movies, maybe never even get into trouble, but she would
live in Paris, and it would go on and on, with endless
adventures. She felt not sleepy, but exhausted.

Krystal Goes Mystical

KRYSTAL, who is normally a happy girl, is talking to her inamorato, Nathan, on the phone. Her voice is barely altered from its usual Queens forthrightness. In fact, if anything, she is even more forthright about the theory she is about to espouse. But it seems as if her voice lowers just a bit, respectfully. Perhaps she is thinking about the last time she went to church—on Christmas Day. Or maybe not. Krystal tells Nathan, "I have this funny feeling. I have the feeling we're both facing something dark and mysterious, some force beyond our control. It's as if we're being tested. And if we can get through this we'll be all right."

Nathan probably agrees with her. He is a good-natured sort, not given to the sulks that Krystal occasionally indulges in. Both of them have confidence in the future; if only they can vanquish the force, prove their mettle, they will no doubt be all right: Nathan will get a well-paying job in the financial community, and Krystal will get the computer programming job that will occupy her until their first baby comes.

But what is this *shmatte*? Nathan wants to know. He is visiting Krystal at her office during lunch-time, and he is dressed in his blue suit: he has just come from a job interview. Nathan has been unemployed for over half a year but draws his daily expenses from a seemingly inexhaustible savings account. Besides, he lives with his parents. (As does Krystal; with her parents, that is.) And he and Krystal have simple tastes. On Friday nights they usually eat at a restaurant in Manhattan, but that is their primary weekend entertainment. And as of late these outings have been somewhat curtailed. Both Nathan and Krystal are on diets. There is good reason for Nathan to cut down: he is stocky, even roly-poly. But Krystal is just what the Germans call good, healthy stock.

But what is remarkable is that Nathan does not know what the *shmatte* is; he does not know this is the tablecloth Krystal has been painstakingly embroidering since junior high school. Or perhaps high school; a long memory is not Krystal's long suit. Nathan did not know Krystal in high school, he only met her two years ago at college, but nevertheless for the past several months Krystal has been hard at work on the tablecloth. It is a dull mustard color, a cloth with a surface both suited to embroidery and water-repellent. Not that Krystal ever intends to eat off this tablecloth; she warns Nathan of this immediately, though she does tell him they'll have to get a dining-room table of the tablecloth's dimensions. "Otherwise all this work will be for nothing," she says.

Of course I could not help overhearing this conversation. I am Krystal's partner. Not a partner of choice, like Nathan; we merely work together, proofreading in a law office. When things are slow Krystal takes out her tablecloth. I have resisted expressing my opinion that the thing is ugly and not worth the trouble. After all, we have to work together, at least until Krystal gets her computer programmer job. But I have difficulty understanding the tablecloth. Why does Krystal spend her time doing it? Because after a while she tires of reading, that's why, and there is not much else to do in our office when things are slow.

Long ago we ran out of things to tell each other, but we still make the effort. I tell her the latest in my complicated love life, though I know she is not at all interested, and she tells me about a life I will only know secondhand.

There is much to envy about Krystal, after all; that much is apparent to anyone who is not as normally happy as she is. She and Nathan will marry in a year or two and live happily; Nathan will make a lot of money in the financial community, though now he is jobless; and Krystal will spend time with the children and her crafts. That will please her, she says. There is no reason to doubt her.

My weekend had been spent in drunkenness and hopeless flirtations; Krystal had helped her parents paint their house. The whole family is, I imagine, exceptionally clean. They are, more or less, Germans. Her father, now working in a bank in some undisclosed capacity, was born in Norway of German parents; her mother was born in Germany of, presumably, German parents as well. But they met in America. That meant (I thought as soon as I heard this tale) that Krystal's mother's family was still in Germany during the war. I have often wondered what Krystal's mother's father, or perhaps her brother, did in the war.

Nathan is Jewish. His parents do not seem to object to his alliance with Krystal, who is, after all, a nice girl, blonde and pretty and sensible. Krystal, for her part, has often been attracted to Jewish boys. I asked her once how they planned to raise their children. I asked as much for guidance as anything else, since I have most often been attracted to blond and blue-eyed men who might well be (like Krystal) Lutheran. Krystal immediately replied that she and Nathan intended to raise any boys they might have as Jewish, for their father, and any girls as Lutheran. The simplicity of this solution stunned me.

I know Krystal disapproves of me. She thinks I lead a fast life. She cannot understand how I can go out on the town until late hours and go home alone; it would no doubt be more understandable, if also more reprehensible, if I did not go home alone. Her world is one of couples. Her most disreputable friend, logically a male, Crazy Todd, has multiple girlfriends, but he only goes out with them one at a time. Crazy Todd and his principal girlfriend, Victoria, often double with Krystal and Nathan. Victoria is a dim-witted girl who thinks only of marriage or, when this seems a pipe dream, an ankle bracelet for Valentine's Day. But what she gets instead for her devotion is the liar and philanderer that Crazy Todd is and admits (to Krystal) he is. Nevertheless Krystal has a sneaking affection for Crazy Todd. Occasionally she has lunch with Victoria, but manages to avoid telling her any of the secrets Crazy Todd has entrusted her with. Her opinion is that Todd only dates Victoria because she is convenient. Victoria lives on Staten Island and likes sex. So does Todd, on both counts. His other girlfriends are more difficult; they live in other boroughs.

Have I mentioned Krystal's soft heart? It is primarily expressed in her tender love for animals, especially those of the stuffed variety, or those rendered on Hallmark cards. The Hallmark shop near the office is one of Krystal's favorite haunts. She is in particular a devotee of the Garfield-the-cat industry, and has managed to make converts of most of her friends, including Nathan. It perplexes her that nothing she can say will endear these cute animals to me.

I tell Krystal I find nothing cute except babies, when I am feeling benevolent. This reminds her of Nathan's

84

grandfather. . . . Nathan's grandfather is senile and is often in Nathan's charge. "He keeps losing his grandfather," Krystal continues. I find this news tantalizing. It takes a while to unravel the story, but it proves to be worth it. Nathan's grandmother, it seems, is in the hospital with a treatable disease. The grandfather has been taken to see her, every day. Every day he wanders off. In the latest episode, he had been found not on the premises at all but in the hospital next door, viewing the newborns.

A phrase from a bad book Krystal recently read (and which I borrowed and read too) floats into my mind: "which added to his confusion, but not his understanding."

Krystal knows her own mind. She has sent out endless letters and resumes; she has steadfastly refused any job offers which consist primarily of typing and answering the phone. "They keep wanting me to be a secretary," she complains, "just because that's what I used to be." I tell her I sympathize; before I reached the level of proofreader the same thing happened to me. We have both been cursed by proficiency at typing. But Krystal is logical; and in the best logic she clearly reasons that the future does not have to be like the past. She does not expect it to be. Why else has she studied computer programming, a career with a future? For better or worse computer programming is her field and she expects to be in it.

On the other hand she is not averse to a little bit of typing. She is willing to make compromises, if the future is bright. This is what worries me. A new, young company has just interviewed her and (Krystal says) told her she seemed "like a good person." A job offer is no doubt imminent, and Krystal is excited by this prospect, though she would have to type a little. Slowly I am beginning to realize that Krystal's days as my partner are numbered, and the thought of her departure fills me with an unexpected dread. It is, after all, hard to find good proofreading partners. And then there is something unsettling, something not very logical, some attachment I feel toward the girl, as if she were my sister. She does, after all, have the same coloring as my sister: blonde hair and blue eyes. And my sister, who lives in California, leads a life not wholly unlike Krystal's: she is traveling along a career path, hoping to make a side trip into matrimony as well.

Unlike my sister, Krystal also knows a lot about my comings and goings. She knows, I sometimes suspect, too much. What she knows, in fact, would make prime blackmail material. As my partner, she is sworn to secrecy, but what might happen if she leaves? And will I begin the same process all over again with her successor?

But the future is not yet at hand. There is still time to prepare my own strategy. I make some discreet inquiries and find that there is nothing much new with Crazy Todd and Victoria. And even if there were, would revealing their secrets threaten Krystal's happiness or peace of mind? It is unlikely. Lately, as a matter of fact, Krystal has not been seeing so much of them; they bore her. Nathan never bores her, she sees him as much as ever, but as far as Nathan is concerned Krystal is under no illusions. He adores her and she knows it and is happy; a slur on Nathan's roly-polyness or his chronic unemployment would probably not rouse her ire. (At least, not until they are married and she cannot escape the responsibility.)

Not, of course, that one would want to make Krystal mad, not even to pierce that inexplicable placidity in the vain hope of finding something behind it. Unless, perhaps, that something might be her parents. . . .

I think often of Krystal's parents. They seem to share a close bond, so close it may be sacred; though Krystal admits there are days when she and her father squabble over the bathroom. She and her mother, on the other hand, are as close as sisters. In fact, Krystal's mother looks so much like Krystal that she thought she recognized herself in Krystal's new passport photo. Does she envy Krystal her forthcoming trip to the Greek Isles? Krystal doesn't think so. She is sure her mother is very happy; her mother's life is very full, she is always keeping busy.

Krystal talks a lot about her mother, perhaps because she spends so much time with her. For some time I have known that, in addition to cooking and cleaning, her mother holds down two unusual jobs: she works in a sweatshop of a knitting mill which produces acrylic sweaters, and she also gives lessons in ceramics in her basement in the evenings.

Her father, though, is something of a dark horse. . . . But under questioning Krystal reveals that his position "in the bank" is that of security guard; he guards the vault in the bank's basement. Nevertheless, he is a short man, stooped and worn from too much hard work (in his youth he was a tailor). Now he sleeps a lot. But he also goes down to his own basement, in the evening, and pours the molds for his wife's cottage industry. After this is done, Krystal tells me, he sits on the bannister and surveys the scene: ten or twelve women hard at work on their ceramics projects. Krystal's father does not say much, but behind his seemingly placid taciturnity he is a good observer, also a practical joker. He watches and waits for somebody to reach a crucial step in the ceramics-making process; then he screams in mock horror. The ceramics-maker, naturally, thinks she has done something wrong; but by the time she has recovered her wits Krystal's father has had a good laugh.

These days this gambit no longer has the desired effect. The workers, all long-term customers, ignore his shrieks, go about their business. But Krystal's father still sits and waits and watches. Recently he played a new joke. For some time he had noticed one woman staring at the ceiling. Her progress with her ceramics project was therefore slow;

and Krystal's mother was not making much money, since the mony comes from new molds, new projects. Krystal's father had a brilliant idea. Before the malingerer's next class he skipped his nap and stole down to the basement. Then, when the class began, he poured the molds as usual and sat on the bannister. Predictably, the woman given to staring at the ceiling looked up at the ceiling, and there she saw a hand-lettered sign that read, What are you looking at the ceiling for?

"So. . . ." Krystal says. She says this a lot. It's a punctuation at the end of her sentences, an intimation of future consequences. It is one of the things about her I found at first irritating but now find endearing. Less endearing is a short, noncommittal laugh she has, somewhere in between a snort and a giggle. I hear it when I tell her something funny or tragic. Krystal has no natural sympathy; she cannot tell the difference. Or perhaps it is really the inflection in my voice which is at fault, my pretense at a jolly cavalier attitude? It is true that, to keep from boring Krystal, I sometimes try to leaven my tales of woe with a little humor, just as I try to vary the timbre of my voice so that these tales are not all delivered in the same flat monotone. But I do not expect, when I mention that perhaps I should kill myself, that she will giggle in the same way as when I talk about my latest office flirtation.

In any case the giggle is not wholly satisfactory. It is merely a polite acknowledgment that Krystal has heard me. What she thinks is another story.

In Krystal's dream she is carrying 100 pounds of dog food to Nathan's house in the Bronx, one 50-pound bag in each hand. (Krystal has strong hands, and likes to keep them busy; thus the tablecloth, and ceramics with her mother, and other crafts.) In another dream, she is lost in the Bronx, looking for Nathan's temple. These episodes were dreamt on the same night; they may have even been parts of the same dream. Both, after all, include Nathan and the Bronx. But then, in one dream she is lost; in the other she is only burdened. Neither of them were really nightmares; but to Krystal's way of thinking, if she stopped to think about it, notwithstanding her strong hands the dog-food dream was probably more frightening.

During the day Krystal often takes naps in our office; but they are too short to dream in. They are just enough to refresh and invigorate; maybe they are too invigorating, because when it is time to go to bed Krystal cannot fall asleep. Amazingly, this is a problem I share; I suggest she take a hot bath at the end of the day. But Krystal takes her bath early in the evening, and is reluctant to change her ways even though she often falls asleep in the tub. When Krystal told me this I was shocked, I thought of her slipping beneath the bubble bath. But Krystal informed me that her bath tub is too shallow, the water does not even reach her shoulders. When she falls asleep she is upright and rigid; there are no dreams to be had in her bath, but no danger either.

Nathan knows this; that is why he is not concerned when she tells him, over the phone, that she fell asleep in her bath last night. She tells him about her dreams, but he does not know what to make of them either, because although he does have a temple he does not have a dog. He does have a cat, one who is openly hostile to Krystal. And Krystal, normally an animal-lover, does not waste her affection on this cat, even though she is Nathan's, because the cat is a rival. It is Krystal's belief that the cat is jealous of Krystal and knows that she, Krystal, will eventually take Nathan away from her, the cat. Meanwhile, they have physical battles in which the cat scratches and Krystal scratches back—or rather, kicks and snarls. After the wedding, Krystal says, she has no intention of bringing the cat into the conjugal home, and Nathan knows it. Krystal has very firm ideas on what will and will not happen after the wedding. The banishment of the cat is one; another is the banishment of Nathan's family, at least on a day-to-day basis. Krystal likes Nathan's family well enough, but she thinks they take advantage of him—they are always thinking up some chore for him to do. This will stop after the wedding as far as Krystal is concerned; they will just have to do without Nathan most of the time.

There is nothing Krystal would like better than a ring on her finger, but she is quite content to let the wedding wait for a year or two. First she has things to do; she has her heart set on the trip to Greece this summer (and she has already sent the tour operator her deposit). And she would also like to go to Aruba again, with her girlfriends, and flirt again with the native boys.

Sometimes you seem younger than me, Krystal told me the other day. But of course this observation did not come out of the blue; I had just confessed, already, that I felt like a teenager. Having found her man, Krystal frankly finds me boy-crazy. But she's used to this; she tells Nathan my life is just like a soap opera, and that interests him, because in these temporary days of his unemployment Nathan has become a soap opera fan. Otherwise it is a mystery what Nathan thinks of me. Krystal does not talk about me much to him, I don't think, although she did say that Nathan was shocked that I was as old as I was. He thought I was about as young as Krystal, if not as innocent. "It's a good thing Nathan has a pot belly," Krystal said the other day, "or I'd be worried you'd try to take him away from me." I assured her that I never attempt to work my charms, seriously, on a friend's beau, to which Krystal gave a surprising response. "But are we friends?" she asked pointedly. I was startled; this kind of challenge was so unlike her. But then Krystal is often surprising me. At that precise moment when she first exhibited her mystical bent (when she mentioned the dark force, on the phone with Nathan), it was so unforeseen that I could not help but exclaim over it. Krystal goes mystical, I said. Krystal laughed her noncommittal laugh.

Are we friends? I told her I didn't know, because I sensed a hidden reproach, or perhaps just a hint of Krystal's true feelings—she may not much like me, really. Yet I profess to my friends, my real friends, that I do indeed like Krystal. And after all these months she does understand me. She knows who I am about to call when I pick up the phone; it is almost a mystical gift. All I can do in a similar vein is tell Nathan's voice from Crazy Todd's; I can also recognize Victoria's plaintive nasal greeting.

Krystal knows other things, too—she knows, for instance, that an investment banker is not my type. One Monday morning I told her all about this date, and my disappointment that I did not fit, or even blend, into his world. I described the dance-room the banker had taken me to, a place filled with young professional men in business suits and their dates—I can't even remember what the girls were wearing. We danced a few numbers. The banker said I made quite a hit, turned heads. But I did not feel at home. I told Krystal all this, and she nodded sympathetically. I never saw so many straight types dancing in one room in my life, I told her; but surprisingly Krystal did not take offense. He's not for you, she said. I recalled how excited she seemed to be, Friday afternoon, when I told her about my date that night; she seemed to think I had maybe finally caught an eligible man. But if she was disappointed on Monday she did not show it.

Krystal is on the phone with Nathan. I have come in at the tail end of a topic; I have just come in with coffee. I settle back and wait for the next topic. Normally I would not be interested in their conversations, but now I am trying to attune myself to peculiarities, mystical overtones.

91

. . . It seems as if Nathan is faced with making a choice. It is one of those difficult choices in life: he must decide between two job prospects, and he must also decide if somebody is lying to him. One job prospect is a solid offer, and Nathan was all ready to accept it, enthusiastically; in fact he has already accepted, though he has not yet started his first day. But now, out of the blue, a personnel agent—one Nathan trusts—has called him up and convinced him to go for an interview someplace else. Worse, the agent has warned him about going to work for the first company, the one whose offer Nathan has already accepted. That place is no good, he told Nathan. You won't last there anyway. There is no future there but a bad one. Three months ago I placed ten people there and within weeks they were all fired. . . . This sounds unpleasant, but plausible; in fact Nathan has already left, by choice or otherwise, two or three jobs in the last mostly-unemployed year. But that's the way it goes in the high-risk commodities business. Given the nature of the business and Nathan's track record, it is amazing that Krystal is so confident that eventually they will be able to afford a house in Westchester County and the loss of her future computer-programmer's salary. This confidence does not accord at all with her logic—or rather with her belief that she is logical. "That's why I majored in computer programming," Krystal says, "because I am logical." At the same time she admits to sometimes indulging in "blonde logic." Under this heading she places all her illogical hopes and funny feelings, like the feeling she has that she will ultimately get a job with Citibank because every personnel agency she has gone to has ended up sending her resume to Citibank—one division or another—and Krystal has already, independently, sent Citibank her resume. "There must be four or five of my resumes floating around Citibank," she said one day, wistfully.

But Nathan's future is more immediate. What will he

do? The second firm, the one Nathan's trusted personnel agent is pushing, is a much more solid prospect. It is not quite what Nathan wants, but it is still more or less in his field (it is still part of the financial community). After much discussion, Krystal and Nathan decide he should go to the interview; but to be on the safe side, Monday morning he will report to the job he has already accepted.

All goes well. Nathan is, eventually, turned down for the job he didn't want anyway. In the meantime, he still has the job he did want. It might be unstable, but so far he hasn't been fired.

The bank wants to get rid of my father, Krystal tells me, because he's getting old and they don't want to pay him a pension. Their excuse is that he stayed home from work one day; but Krystal's father has a good reason for that. They were painting the vault, and the paint fumes gave him a headache. He did not want his headache to get worse, so he stayed home the next day and slept.

I thought about the weekend Krystal's family painted their house and slept there, as usual; but I was afraid to ask why those paint fumes did not bother her father. Perhaps because they were his own paint fumes. Krystal's family feels secure in their house in Queens; they never worry that the kiln in the basement will explode, for instance, nor about the character of the strangers who invade their home every evening for the ceramics sessions. There is not much real danger in my neighborhood, either, and my acquaintances are for the most part normal, but nevertheless I hesitate about inviting Krystal to my apartment. She would never understand the necessity of living with cockroaches and crumbling plaster. Dirty walls bother Krystal; I know this because she has often remarked that the walls in our office, which seem only mildly dingy to me, are disgusting and in urgent need of a paint job. I tell her I wish fixing up my place were so simple, but before my walls could be painted they would have to be replastered. "It's so bad it would take a week to fix it," I tell Krystal, "and where would I sleep in the meantime?" Krystal does not laugh at this; it is clear she thinks this is no excuse. A week is not very long in the grand design of Krystal's life; she plans ahead, arranges logistics for parties and weddings weeks ahead, keeps in mind her own wedding even though it is years away. . . . For my part, I think it is a shame that since I broke up with my last boyfriend I have no reliable alternative place to stay. This, I am sure, would never occur to Krystal, who would never move in with Nathan on such a casual basis—not even to escape paint fumes.

Now the tablecloth is finished—Krystal has finished it. In honor of the occasion I come around to her side of the table and finger its embroidered folds. The water-repellent surface is softer than it looks. Krystal announces her intention of giving the thing to her mother. After all that work? I ask, thinking of Krystal's future home with Nathan. Well, says Krystal, there's no guarantee I'll ever have a table just this size. If I do, my mother will probably let me have it back.

I congratulate Krystal, but in my heart I feel only dread, and not at the prospect of the tablecloth's eventual display on Krystal's mother's table in Queens. That was no doubt inevitable, given Krystal's fondness for her mother, and her lack of a table of her own. The feeling I have is also inevitable, inescapable—a funny, illogical feeling, but a sure feeling all the same: Krystal will be leaving me shortly. There is no longer any reason for her to stay here.

All along, of course, I have hoped that secretly Krystal was reluctant to leave. But what have I based this on? Merely the fact that this law firm has been part of her life for three years (in her college days she worked here part-time as a secretary), and nobody likes to leave the known for the unknown—I know I don't. And then again, there was Krystal's future trip to Greece. Here she was assured of enough time to go to Greece; in a new job she might not be granted a summer vacation. I heard her tell Nathan once, on the phone, that she might just put off her job hunt until after she'd been to Greece. But now I see that this was just bravado. It's true that Krystal has set her heart on the trip, and she doesn't like to change her plans; but it's also true, even truer, that nothing depresses her so profoundly as her failure to find a suitable job. That must mean a suitable job makes all the difference to her happiness and well-being, even more than the chance of adventure and flirtation in distant lands.

But now the tablecloth is done. She had hoped to finish it by Christmas, and now it is many months past Christmas. The tablecloth is long overdue and so is Krystal's departure; even though the young, eager company who interviewed her recently did reject her in the end, there must be another young, eager company who is only too glad to have somebody like Krystal; the end is coming soon.

When Nathan sees the tablecloth on Krystal's mother's table, does he feel a surge of affection for its creator, a desire to give her a home of her own? If he does he probably does not tell Krystal, or at least I do not hear of it. He does tell Krystal he is sorry he called it a *shmatte*, it was just that when he first laid eyes on it, it was crumpled up in an office chair—it was not displayed to its best advantage.

On an impulse, I phone my sister in California, just to see how she's doing. She says she's fine, but tired. Idly I ask her the name of the hospital she works at. She is surprised I don't already know, and so am I; but it never occurred to me to ask. It is a very famous hospital, "the hospital of the stars." I can't help being impressed—my sister gets to see celebrities in wheelchairs. But she's used to that. Unfortunately, she rarely meets any eligible doctors, though she does see them rushing about their rounds.

95

I ask my sister about her love life, but she has nothing new to tell me. Although she habitually goes to temple dances and answers personal ads in singles magazines (unlike me, my sister would never dream of picking up men in bars), currently she is dating nobody. This is because she's just too busy—she is taking two graduate courses in her field, health care management, at night, and what with classes and homework, not to mention dispatching nurses all day long, she is dead. Her exhaustion is so all-encompassing that when I mention that my ex-boyfriend, an attractive Englishman whom she has never met, will be vacationing in L.A. soon, she tells me that she has no time to see him. I feel a grudging respect for my sister, who can so easily turn down an adventure if she suspects it might be worthless.

At work the next day I tell Krystal about the phone call with my sister. She's far away, but reassuringly there, and still my sister, I tell Krystal. Krystal does not seem to understand. I remember that Krystal is an only child; she could not be expected to understand. It must be strange, I say aloud, to be an only child. Naturally, Krystal bridles at this. Never having had a sister, naturally she would find this entirely normal, not strange. Not strange, says Krystal, echoing my thoughts.

After a moment she concedes that perhaps she does, occasionally, miss having a sister. I think of the picture Krystal has painted of her family—an Old World family— and find myself wondering aloud why her parents never chose to have more children.

There is a silence. I have a funny feeling, a premonition of dread. I have asked the wrong question. . . . But it is even worse than I fear. Krystal replies: I had a sister . . . but she died.

She says this in a flat tone, not the tone of tragedy. But if there is no place for personal tragedy in Krystal's life, in her voice there is a warning. It wasn't meant to be, Krystal adds; and I don't dare ask anything else.

Not long after this, Krystal takes a day off to go to three job interviews. The odds are finally too great. When she returns the next day, she announces she has a job. I take the news calmly; I have been preparing. Now I know that there are only two weeks left.

The deadline is firmly established in my mind; but oddly, Krystal does not seem to act as if the end is near. For all her advance planning, she lives in the present quite nicely; she trudges in to work each day, a victim of her usual sleepiness, grumbling about our work or our lack of it, as if she expected the situation to continue indefinitely. At the same time she does not seem as happy as I expected; for a day she was euphoric enough, but after that she calmed down. Perhaps now that the future is in clear view it does not seem quite real to her.

There are a few things Krystal would like to do before she goes: she would like to finish the bad novel I have lent her (though I would be only too happy to let her take it with her when she leaves); she would also like to sample the cheese and spinach soufflé at the bar I frequent at lunch-time, and stock up on toiletries at the local discount drugstore. For my part, I ask her to draw me a map of the law firm; though I have been here almost a year, she has been here longer, and knows its maze-like mysteries far better. After she is gone, after all, I will have nobody to give me directions—at least nobody who will not laugh at me for getting lost.

How is Nathan's grandfather? I ask her one day. Still senile? It was meant to be a joke, in a way, but Krystal answered me seriously. No, he's been much better, she said. Ever since his wife got out of the hospital. I knew he'd be all right once he got her back. Except. . . .

Except? I prompted.

Except now Nathan's grandmother is back in the hospital, Krystal said. It's her heart again; and who knows what will happen to his grandfather now.

97

I plan Krystal's going-away party. We will have an open house; all of Krystal's friends, and mine, will be invited to drop in. Our friends at the firm do not necessarily coincide, but that's all right. She will suffer the lawyers I flirt with, and I will make the best of the company of the messengers and supply clerks who adore Krystal. Krystal enjoys the adoration of these men, and does flirt with them, despite her attachment to Nathan. Sometimes this worries me, but she has an iron-clad retort: she only flirts with messengers and supply clerks because she knows they are safe. Whether or not they know this is another question. One messenger, a very forward sort, has already asked her repeatedly to lunch. I wonder if Krystal is playing with fire, and if so, if I have had anything to do with it. Perhaps she has heard too many tales from me, of how I have broken the rules against interoffice fraternization with seeming impunity. But she knows that in one case, my fooling around was not really fooling around at all—it had consequences. Krystal does not want any consequences; yet elderly messengers grab her in the hall, lunch invitations are constant—it's a good thing she is leaving.

In the days that are left I study Krystal with a new eye. She now habitually wears makeup, at least blue eyeshadow and eyeliner and lipstick. Way back when, when we first met, she refused to be bothered with such paint; she didn't think it was fun; she probably thought she was young enough not to need it anyway. But ten months have gone by. Krystal has turned twenty-two. She still does not bother with any foundation, but she does wear the eyeshadow and the liner and the lipstick, and she looks great. At least I think so; Nathan, Krystal tells me, doesn't mind it, but he really likes her *au naturel*.

Yes; it is a good thing Krystal is leaving, leaving me, before I can corrupt her further. At the same time I wonder if perhaps she hasn't corrupted me; for I have gone out again with the investment banker, to dinner this time, and to my surprise I enjoyed myself immensely.

Krystal is a picky eater. She has told me this, and this is what I remember when I am in the grocery store trying to pick out what to buy for her farewell party. Once Krystal rattled off a whole list of foods she wouldn't eat. I forget most of them, but I do remember what Krystal told me one day when both of us were drinking orange juice, for our health. "Nathan would approve of this," she said, "he's always trying to get me to drink orange juice. I told him he'd won, I liked orange juice now, but he'd never get me to balance string beans on my nose." This is the only epigram I ever heard Krystal utter; it is so obscure, even mystical, that it might well be an epitaph. I ventured to say I didn't understand. "Nathan didn't either, at first," replied Krystal. "It means I'll never eat vegetables; at least I'll never like them."

It is Monday morning and I am alone in the office. Though I left Friday night in a hurry, there are no remnants of our party left. Somebody, mysteriously, has cleaned up over the weekend. . . . But as of yet I do not have a new partner. Across town, Krystal (I imagine) is undergoing her first day at the new job; no doubt it has already obliterated, in her mind, this job. This job, for Krystal, must only be a shadow, a slightly unreal past. Luckily, Krystal can look forward to the future.

Because it is Monday I feel my usual restlessness, a need to relate the triumphs and horrors of the weekend, a desire to plan aloud my hopes and schemes for the coming week—I only plan ahead by the week. But of course there is nobody to listen. Perhaps that is for the best. Too much restlessness is, after a certain age, not truly productive. It dissipates one's energy, energy that could be used for more important things than hopes and schemes. Perhaps I should learn how to use a computer.

In the meantime, the silence seems to bounce off the walls. It is not like Krystal's silence. But the walls remind me of Krystal; not dingy, like she found them, just blank. I study the walls, the ceiling. Never would I want to be Krystal; but it might be nice to be like her, to be as happy as she is, or at least as normal. . . . But is even Krystal normal? I think of her family: their secret, unspoken tragedy, the sacrifice of her mother's life, the practical jokes of her father that have, practically speaking, no purpose. I'm looking at the walls, I'm looking at the ceiling—but what am I looking at the ceiling for? It's not, after all, heaven. Before I can go mystical, I turn on the radio for company.

Trixie Taylor, Hospital Nurse

FROM their hospital beds they listen patiently to tinkling, tittering noises down the hall, rising through the corridor like a party in progress. Is it some celebration for the recovery of a fortunate unknown patient, or is it the secret they suspect—the cocktail hour in the doctors' lounge, presided over by Trixie Taylor, Hospital Nurse?

Cockroaches in the old building, flies in the new wing: Trixie Taylor has been transferred. Her gaiety at all times, even after hours on the graveyard shift, tended to depress the old building's old and infirm patients. In the new wing, there are younger men and women in bed. The men, believing all the legends of the accessibility of pretty nurses, mull over plans to seduce Trixie Taylor in the not too distant future. Accessibility, the men think. Accessibility of a sink, think the women. All the women patients in the new wing, those who are coiffed and those who are not coiffed—all the women, their heads crushed by coarse pillows, admire Trixie's hairdo, a shining Dutch bob. And yet neither the men nor the women see Trixie Taylor very often. It is enough that her laughter floats irresistibly from the nurses' station, irresistible and loud enough to reach five or six semi-private rooms in either direction. Her laugh conjures the required visions: the

103

bells of passion, or clean fine streams of water dripping from her healthy head. . . .

Trixie Taylor is one of our best nurses, does it matter she was once a nightclub singer? joked one orderly to another. The orderlies were standing in a closet. They often joked as they fluffed bed linens and inventoried hospital supplies. But as neither had a pipeline to the hospital administrators, their little joke meant nothing.

And the doctors, where did they stand in this debate over Trixie and the reasons for her transfer? Hospital doctors, for the most part surgeons, are not inclined to joke much, but they do enjoy a challenge, or else they would not spend night and day in the endless rounds and operations of the hospital. They would instead be presiding over a busy but comfortable suburban practice, aided by Linda Taylor—Trixie's sister.

Linda Taylor, Office Nurse, spends most of her day processing Blue Cross forms, but after work she goes to a new cocktail lounge in the suburbs that has become popular for its exotic South Seas drinks. Occasionally she invites Trixie to join her, but Trixie invariably declines the invitation. Linda understands: for sisters and fellow-nurses they are very different types. Linda Taylor, Office Nurse, suspects that beneath Trixie's gaiety is the understandable depression usually found in the kind of girl who becomes a Hospital Nurse. It's a different world, thinks Linda over her Mai Tai: her walls are gray, but mine are white, and washed and painted regularly.

Is it true that Trixie Taylor was once a nightclub singer? the doctors ask each other. A rumor is floating about the hospital. It is an intriguing rumor, so intriguing that, for a moment, Stanley Seagram's attention was diverted from the body on the operating table in front of him. During that time Dr. Stanley Seagram, a surgeon known for his imagination, imagined Trixie in sequins, smoke in his eyes. Then he got back to the bloody business at hand. Afterwards, recalling a scene from a Mamie Van Doren movie he had seen in the fifties, Stanley was able to imagine Trixie Taylor in more detail as a Nightclub Singer. He had little difficulty picturing himself removing Trixie's hospital whites (an easy operation, if one could believe the other doctors) and then encasing her in a sequined costume ending in a mermaid's tail.

When he told this tale to his fellow surgeons, they were all suitably impressed by the mermaid's tail, an imaginative touch.

Why are there younger patients in the new wing? Trixie wondered soon after her transfer. She telephoned Linda Taylor, Office Nurse. Linda, who knew nothing about the hospital, hazarded a guess: the younger patients had better Blue Cross. Trixie Taylor hated filling out forms, and even though she had little to do with insurance she was now in charge of patient lists and medical histories. Linda Taylor, who had heretofore thought the only advantages of the new wing were younger patients and flies instead of cockroaches, told Trixie she ought to complain. Why should a good Hospital Nurse like you have to bother with paperwork? she asked smugly. She was always the smarter sister; she understood the logic, the hidden intricacies and secret meanings of medical insurance. Trixie explained that she couldn't complain: it was a promotion. She was now in charge of giving patients their pills. "And shots too?" Linda asked eagerly. "No, another nurse is in charge of giving shots," Trixie said. She didn't mind not giving shots, because the patients who needed shots were usually in grave pain and not good company.

But most of the patients in the new wing are not seriously ill. They have a future to look forward to, an office to work in. Before Trixie Taylor arrived, they longed for the sounds of normal life, of piped-in music in elevators and in the offices of doctors they will visit when they are healthy. Linda Taylor, Office Nurse, does not even notice the music in her office. Mood music is subtle, you only notice it when it stops. In the new wing's semi-private rooms the patients used to dream about mood music, but they have stopped. Instead, they imagine they hear party music. . . .

Dr. Stanley Seagram, who is more interested in mermaids than nurses, notices a cocktail lounge called the South Seas not too far from the hospital. Inside he finds the waitresses are not, as he had hoped, mermaids, but only the more predictable island-maiden type. They wear long, full grass skirts. He goes to the bar and drinks morosely, trying to imagine himself attracted to island girls, but the liquor only depresses him. He can think of nothing but mermaids. After several drinks he gets up to go to the men's room, and on his way he collides with a woman coming out of the ladies' room. She is wearing a long, tight-fitting green dress of some material Stanley imagines to be Spandex or Lurex. It is Linda Taylor, Office Nurse.

Hospital hygiene is not what it could be, the orderlies agree. They are not talking about the shade of the walls or the bed linen or even the insect problem, but the grooming habits of most of the nurses on their floor. All of these nurses (the orderlies joke) are pimply or slovenly, and only Trixie Taylor, despite all odds, is capable of inspiring visions of good health. Is that why (the orderlies wonder) the other nurses do not seem especially fond of Trixie Taylor?

The orderlies are still standing in a closet, but the closet adjoins a semi-private room and the gray wall in between is thin. One of Trixie's patients, a young man, hears the orderlies' joke and thinks, That's the truth. He speculates that the other nurses are never invited into the doctors' lounge. They are bound to be jealous of Trixie Taylor and therefore disinclined to laugh with her. Then who is Trixie Taylor laughing with? The patient imagines it must be the doctors, but he is wrong. What passes for a cocktail party to a patient who cannot get out of bed is only the noise that passes for mood music to a hospital worker—before noon, the rounds of medical students and breakfast carts; after noon, the comings and goings of parties of visitors.

But what about the doctors' lounge? The truth is that the doctors' lounge is nowhere near Trixie Taylor's nurses' station. It is a long trip through winding corridors and hidden freight elevators. Linda Taylor, knowing nothing about the hospital and always getting lost in it, would have trouble finding the doctors' lounge, but Trixie knows very well where it is.

Could that be Trixie Taylor's private joke? Because the truth is, Trixie Taylor is only laughing to herself.

Linda Taylor, Office Nurse, does not think of herself that way. After work she is Linda Taylor, Girl About Town. She owns more Girl About Town costumes than nurse's uniforms. All nurses in uniform look alike, thinks Linda, and why look like a nurse when the South Seas is full of nurses in uniform? A girl about town needs a different costume every night to get noticed. That is why Linda Taylor disappears into the South Seas ladies' room dressed as a nurse and emerges looking like a nightclub singer. Because nightclub singers do not carry bundles, she leaves her nurse's gear under the sink where another girl about town—resourceful, imaginative, also needing a new costume for the night—finds it. That is the real reason Linda Taylor has more evening gowns than nurse's uniforms.

The hospital administrators have a private joke. They are the only ones who know the real reason for Trixie Taylor's transfer. A ward of old women suspects the truth, but. . . . Although the hospital administrators and the orderlies have never actually met, the administrators have a pipeline to the orderlies' gossip. It is a secret vent in the supply closet. In the doctors' lounge, it is merely a matter of employing spies. The hospital administrators are resourceful, well-organized. But they do not like public jokes. Efficiently they spread the new gossip: Trixie Taylor is no nightclub singer. Trixie Taylor, who has been transferred to the new wing, has never been a nightclub singer. She has been promoted. Hospital administrators would not promote a former nightclub singer. The hospital administrators plotted this argument carefully, knowing that in the logic of gossip only the illogical is passed on. Soon nobody believes that Trixie was ever a nightclub singer, not even Dr. Stanley Seagram, now that he believes in mermaids.

Where is the hospital? It is not far from the South Seas. It is not in a dangerous neighborhood. If hospital nurses and doctors live dangerously, it has nothing to do with the neighborhood. Everything happens indoors, in lounges designed for doctors and cocktails. The only nurses on the streets are Visiting Nurses. . . .

What kind of girl wants to be a Visiting Nurse? Linda Taylor once asked Trixie in passing. Someone who has a dull fiancé, Trixie replied. Linda had completely forgotten that years ago, in her nursing school days, Trixie had planned to marry the boy next door and then go off to new neighborhoods as a Visiting Nurse. (Secretly, Trixie found her fiancé dull. She looked forward to the adventure of visiting other people's houses every day.) But the fiancé put his foot down. Too dangerous. Stay in the hospital.

What kind of girl ends up a Hospital Nurse? Trixie asked

herself, soon after she was promoted. A nurse looking for a husband? For the first time in years Trixie Taylor thought about the dull fiancé she had escaped marrying. The hospital is my husband, Trixie thinks. But perhaps a dull husband these days. She laughs suddenly, dangerously.

What passes for a cocktail party to a ward of old women in the old building is only the normal mood music a doctor and a nurse make together. . . . The ward of old women is located just down the hall from the doctors' lounge. In the days when Trixie Taylor was their Ward Nurse, before she was transferred, the old women used to listen to disturbing laughter issuing from the doctors' lounge. The old women suspected the disturbing laughter was Trixie's, but they could prove nothing. Usually they only heard the sound in their sleep, and when they awoke, Trixie was already in the ward with them—not laughing, but whispering. In a soft, coaxing voice she asked them questions: How are you today? she would start with. But before the women could describe their present mood she was asking them peculiar questions about their pasts, things they didn't want to think about anymore. What was your secret wish? Your worst nightmare? What games did you play as a child? What did you do in the war?

How dangerous is Trixie Taylor? Too dangerous, thought her ex-fiancé. (He suspected her of rifling his drawers and reading his letters. There was nothing she did not know about him! It was no wonder she found him dull.)

How funny, the hospital administrators thought, that old women, who normally will talk to anybody who will listen, complain that Trixie Taylor asks too many questions. They took the complaint seriously.

In the new wing, Trixie Taylor is laughing over her

files. It is the tinkling, tittering noise her new patients find so attractive. It is louder than her old whisper, but more subtle. Behind her new desk Trixie has learned to be more subtle, more imaginative. She has learned to read between the lines of medical records. Her patients are too young to have real histories, but they have jobs. On her desk are the names and occupations of these new patients, the ones she gives pills to but rarely visits. Trixie does not have to visit them. In her imagination she floats down the corridor into each semi-private room. She puts herself in each bed and thinks about the life she will lead when she leaves the hospital. In each bed she has a new job to look forward to: Trixie Taylor, Policewoman; Trixie Taylor, Fashion Model; Trixie Taylor, Attorney-at-Law; Trixie Taylor, Business Executive. Occasionally there are other Trixies not found in any of the semi-private rooms: Trixie Taylor, Secret Agent; Trixie Taylor, Nightclub Singer; Trixie Taylor, Visiting Nurse.

In the old building, the old women are again hearing disturbing laughter from the doctors' lounge. Trapped in their beds, they imagine it is Trixie, their worst nightmare. But the laughter they find disturbing is normal and healthy. It is only a visitor to the hospital, a party for Dr. Stanley Seagram. It is Linda Taylor, Office Nurse, who knows very well where she is.

110

Etiology of the New War

YEARS WENT BY before the time was ripe for the New War. Then balances dropped. There I was at the bank, waiting for my chance to drop my balance.

A practical joke started me thinking seriously about the New War. It all started as a practical joke. Who plays practical jokes these days at banks? Only lunatics. People are serious about their money these days.

So it wasn't a practical joke any more than it was really a bank robbery.

After hours the bank is a Money Machine. The Machine is always pleasant and obliging, except when it is having a breakdown. In that case one has only to pick up the 24-hour phone and report the breakdown to whomever is standing by.

The best disguise for a bank-lunatic is a bona fide bank card. She waved it around to establish her credentials. Then she leisurely walked up to the 24-hour phone and cried into it, "Hurry! Bank robbery! Bank robbery!"

Only two people had any presence of mind. One was the lunatic herself, who then reported the exact location of our bank. The other was a man who came forward immediately to contradict her statement. He said to the phone, "This woman has a problem." Then he turned to the rest of us and said, "There isn't anybody there anyway."

It is no good having presence of mind when there is no presence at the other end of a 24-hour phone.

"Don't you like practical jokes?" the woman with a problem inquired. "Don't you like practical jokes?"

"No!"

"This man has no sense of humor," she announced. "No sense of humor. This man has no sense of humor."

She started grinning. "THIS MAN has no sense of humor!"

She kept grinning until she realized she was angry.

I wondered, what has this woman got to do with the New War?

Points of Possible Comparison:
   The New War is a false alarm.
   The New War is a joke.
   Will the New War bring excitement into the lives of potential fools, heroes, voyeurs?

Of course the New War is an idea whose time has come, but it is still only an idea. The place has not yet been settled. We all know the befores and the afters, the etiology and the consequences, but where? Popular opinion says the Middle East. The climate there is volatile. But what of the climate of the Middle West? This season, a definite absence of snow. Anything can happen in a winter lacking its usual wonderland.

Wondering about things, even casually, while standing in a bank line, can be dangerous. Things creep in from nowhere and get named before they are even understood. What the hell did I mean by the New War? I asked myself in retrospect. It was only after that it occurred to me to wonder about before. Because right then and there in the

bank the New War seemed so old that it had already re-
ceded into the background. It was so much more exciting
to wonder about other roles this practical-joking woman
might someday play—in espionage, communications, mil-
itary intelligence. I asked myself, what will this woman
get to do in the New War?

Nobody is sure what the New War is, but if we watch
the nightly news we can discover its etiology. On television, history predicts itself. We are all waiting for the
New War, but we are afraid it is going to let us down
when it finally shows up.

Advance preparation may be the only way to see any
action. But the New War demands new boots. I bought a
new pair of old 60's go-go boots, the kind I never had in
those days, and went walking down the street. I was talking too much and suddenly I fell.

What do all the cripples on the streets of New York have
to do with the New War? They must be the consequences of
the New War, though it has not yet begun. They're ahead of
their time. These a priori consequences are not to be confused with causes. Cripples don't start wars. The etiology of
the New War must be found elsewhere. Where?

Falling on the street can have serious consequences.
One bone breaks easily into six pieces. Where? The
kneecap. The worst place for a break. Bioenergetic theory
has it that tension accumulates in the knee. The serious
consequences of such tension breaking up are ten weeks in
the Middle West, in a time remarkable for its absence of
winter wonderland.

In a big city of the Middle West in the middle sixties, a
girl on her way to school was shot at, but the bullet hit
her powder compact. Her life was thus prolonged indefinitely.

Presumably the powder compact exploded. Where did
the powder go?

Going to the bank used to be such a predictable thing. Usually all would go well. Occasionally there would be a bank robbery. This was also predictable, or at least understandable. Now it is necessary to dream up new approaches to the predictable. Practical jokes at the bank are new and unpredictable. But are they fun? Would only a lunatic think it just as much fun reporting a stickup that never happened?

The funny thing is, though what I witnessed was only the *idea* of a bank robbery, I was left with a distinct impression of horror—similar, I would guess, to the horror people used to feel after a real bank robbery.

What does the lunatic have to do with the New War? In the bank I was too horror-struck to wonder any such thing. It was only after that I began putting the pieces together. But did I really think about what uses the government might make of that poor crazy woman in the War? Of course not. The New War was not yet real. I was still nursing my old wounds. I was still thinking in old ways. Poor crazy woman. Symptom of our times. Cause (at least partial) of the New War. You can see how my thinking went. In old ways, old patterns. Confusion of the symptom and the cause. Symptoms are one thing; etiology is another. Consequences are the reality!

What does the lunatic have to do with the New War? Sometimes the answer is hidden in the past. The end is lurking in the beginning. Every story has a beginning, but the beginning is not always told. In the beginning, the lunatic ran into the bank and cried, "Thank you! Thank you for letting me in!" Then she began snorting in a peculiar way. Or was it laughing?

Then there was a lull. We waited without knowing what we were waiting for. She was getting her big break.

We thought it was peace. How were we to know she was a lunatic?

The absence of normal thought can be dangerous. The absence of normal tension can also be dangerous. These conditions exist in the Middle West regardless of the weather.

When the New War comes will it be an anticlimax?

In the Middle West I lay on my bed, thinking about romance and adventure. My dangerous go-go boots were hidden away in a corner of the room. I didn't want to throw them out yet. Possibly someday I would get brave enough to put them on again. All ideas seemed possible, for the future. Such plans I had for my return to normalcy! After ten weeks I was back in New York. The time was ripe. What did I do? I went to the bank.

Going to the bank is now an everyday occurrence. One day I met a lunatic, but the next I met a friend. Actually he is only an acquaintance. We met at a party, long ago. He talked about both of us going to see a psychic he knows. We made plans, but nothing happened. I went walking in my go-go boots and the rest is history.

Now everything is changed. I am back on my feet, looking where I am going and not talking so much. The New War is coming. I wonder if, this time, my acquaintance will really make an appointment for me with the psychic. Or was he only joking? I plan to ask the psychic about my future prospects for romance and adventure and, incidentally, money. If there's time after all that, I might ask, What have I got to do with the New War?

A Murder History

OUTSIDE DETROIT, in a wooded suburb, a killer came to visit a young woman who had a baby—only the baby was not there and the killer did not kill.

As it turned out, the killer (or criminal) and the young woman had attended the same elementary school in Detroit—he in the fifties, she in the sixties. At these times there had been a world of difference between them. When he was a sixth-grader—already wearing patent-leather hair, shoes to match—she was a baby. And when she was a sixth-grader, he was grown, past his juvenile delinquency, a young man who looked like an old man, so many crimes had he already committed.

Stealing tires, hubcaps, cars, that kind of thing, that was what most of his crimes were. The killing was accidental—a one-time shot, a robbery of a liquor store—and though he had never been caught for that crime, the criminal had spent several sleepless nights worrying about it.

Murder was not his style.

For a while after that successful liquor-store holdup (and unsolved murder) the criminal, Bobby was his name, went straight. He married a girl from another city who knew nothing about his past. The girl taught music, a funny thing Bobby thought, since he had never liked music, not even rock and roll, and even more he had never liked his teachers. Most of them, in that school in Detroit, were quite old in the fifties. Mostly they were old maids who never fathomed what any of their young students were up to. Because Bobby wasn't the only one who was a young criminal in those days, the neighborhood being what it was (white lower-middle-class) and the times also being what they were, the school was full of twelve-year-old juvenile delinquents.

By the time the girl began going to the school, in the early sixties, the ranks of what was known in the neighborhood as the Woods Gang (because gang members smoked cigarettes and plotted crimes in a nearby woods) had thinned. Those in the Gang had graduated to junior high school, high school, and beyond. Some of the girl's babysitters—for instance, the babysitter who teased her hair and set it in front of the TV—still ran with boys who looked as though they might belong to the Gang. The girl and her sister and her brother didn't like this babysitter and often reported to their parents her crime of spilling hair-setting lotion on the living-room carpet. But really it wasn't hair-setting lotion, only water.

Only once did the babysitter commit a more serious crime in everyone's eyes, which was letting one of her boyfriends, a JD type, come over and visit her while she was on the job. He didn't come into the house, they met secretly in some bushes, but that was bad enough. The children told their mother and the babysitter was not called anymore. Because in the mid-sixties in Detroit, in fact all over the midwest, murders were being committed for no reason and everybody was afraid.

These murders in the midwest in the mid-sixties were mostly murders done by maniacs in the night. Houses and cottages were broken into and somebody was shot at, or strangled. Often whole families were killed. There were several of these mass murders in those times.

Of course the more sensational headlines were reserved

for those cases involving a senator's daughter, seven student nurses (both in the midwest) and a sniper in Tucson (not the midwest, a forerunner of crimes to come, moving out to the west).

Funny how the young woman, too, when she looked back on her childhood in Detroit, remembered these more sensational crimes even though they were not exactly what had frightened her. What frightened her were some crimes she could not really remember, murders that seemed to happen all the time in Michigan and Illinois and Indiana. For some reason she fixed on Indiana as the most sinister place of all. She had never been to Indiana.

Even though the young woman's mother fired the babysitter it was not really because she thought the babysitter's boyfriend would murder her children. She only thought it wasn't proper behavior for a babysitter to display, making secret assignations in the bushes when her young charges were left in their beds to suffer alone the nightmares of childhood.

The nightmares of adolescence were yet to come, and when they came, a couple of years later, the young woman who was only thirteen and on the brink of something used to wake up and imagine there was an intruder in the house.

But since the babysitter's black-leather-jacketed boyfriend never came into the house, the intruder of the girl's waking nightmares became a man who lived in the basement and prowled the house, several nights a week. Several nights a week the girl lay awake, expecting to be murdered in her bed.

Everybody blamed her nightmares on adolescence but really the girl had been expecting to be murdered in her bed for years. Although elementary-school children in those days were not so well-informed, they knew about President Kennedy and they knew about murders.

By this time the teachers in the school were not so old as they had been in Bobby's day. Many of the old maids had died—natural deaths—and had been replaced by younger and more modern teachers. The old maids who were still alive often had student teachers to help them. The girl remembered a Miss Zipper of 1963.

Miss Zipper had not won a 1963 zipper contest; that was her real name. Except it might have been Miss Zipser after all.

Another teacher with a funny name was Miss Bells, the music teacher. Miss Bells was not her real name, the young woman did remember the music teacher's real name and it did have something to do with bells, but since Miss Bells may still be living her innocence must be protected.

Miss Bells, being the music teacher, never had a student teacher to help her, only lots of old song books with ageless tunes like "Waltzing Matilda." She was a very tall, thin woman with rhinestone glasses on a chain and hair dyed an unnatural coppery red. Looking back on her memory's picture of Miss Bells, the young woman decided she must have used a good deal of pancake makeup to achieve the effect of her skin, a velvety surface bulging at the jowls. No wrinkles, so it was impossible to guess her age.

Miss Bells, though the music teacher, did not have much to do with putting on the annual Christmas pageant, which was a school-wide performance directed by the auditorium teachers (teachers who taught in the auditorium, whatever subjects couldn't be taught in a classroom). Miss Bells was, however, the director of the Glee Club and she did conduct the Christmas concert. These memories had no resonance at all for the young woman, since "Waltzing Matilda" was all she remembered from her music classes. Except that it seemed that it was at Christmas time, a particularly sentimental time of year for Miss Bells, that she took out a scrapbook of mementos and photographs and told her class something that the young woman never forgot.

Only once had Miss Bells ever shown her photographs and told her story, one Christmas, in 1964 or 1965.

2

When Bobby rang the doorbell of the young woman's house in the Detroit suburb and she saw him dressed in a black leather jacket, she was not alarmed.

In the years since the fifties black leather had come back into style. In fact the young woman, before returning to Detroit, had lived in New York and worn black leather too. She, unlike Bobby—whose era it belonged to—liked rock and roll.

Since those modern years in New York things had changed for her. She had gotten married and had a baby at the same time that Bobby's wife left him and he went back to a life of crime.

A life of crime, Bobby thought, it sounds so easy and yet it's not. Because now that he was grown up he had to make a living out of a life of crime.

Times are hard for everyone in Detroit now but it is still true that outside Detroit proper, in the suburbs, live some people with things to steal.

Bobby did not come to steal from the young woman, or he would not have been dressed in his black leather jacket. When he was working he wore a moving-man's outfit, along with the rest of his gang. Actually Bobby lived not far from the young woman, in a neighboring suburb which was almost as affluent as hers. It wasn't easy being a moving-man criminal but it did pay.

This particular day Bobby wasn't working, just riding his motorcycle like the old days. Then something went wrong with it and he needed to call a service station.

The young woman let him in because she was no longer afraid for herself, having lived in New York and played at being tough, and finding out that people believed how tough she looked. Her baby was at nursery school—the baby was not really a baby any longer, any more than the killer was really a killer these days—so she was not alarmed. Even though her husband was away at work and not there to protect her she did not worry about being raped, since it had never happened to her and since rape had not been in the headlines when she was a child, only murder.

Bobby only wanted to use her telephone, but he figured that while he was in the house he might as well look it over, in case he wanted to pull a job on his own some night, a burglary. It did not enter his mind to rape her either, because he had never raped anybody, and because when he was a kid stealing had been his style of crime and still was.

There was in fact a huge gap between the criminal and the young woman, though at first they didn't realize it, since they were now both adults and ten years between adults doesn't seem like much. Especially since Bobby, this particular criminal, had outgrown his old-man look and become quite youthful-looking, especially when he was out riding his motorcycle. And the young woman, like most young women, had aged since having her baby.

The gas station Bobby called about fixing his motorcycle told him he had to wait awhile, and since he had to kill time, she offered him a cup of coffee.

Most strangers, meeting casually, do not ask about each other's pasts, but Bobby, to allay suspicions he thought she might have, told her that he was her neighbor, almost. She said one suburb wasn't the same as the next, and then changed her mind and said yes, they were all the same, and that she was proud of having grown up in Detroit proper. And he said he'd lived in Detroit proper too when he was a kid and they compared notes and found they'd both gone to the same elementary school.

So we were neighbors, they concluded, not yet thinking of the difference between his neighborhood and hers (the years, the declining importance of the Woods Gang in terrorizing that neighborhood).

Bobby was before Miss Zipser's time but he did remember many of the old-maid teachers who had survived into the sixties to teach the young woman. In particular Bobby remembered Miss Bells because his estranged wife was also a music teacher.

The young woman told Bobby a story about Miss Bells.

3

One Christmas Miss Bells took out her photograph albums and showed us pictures of all her former classes. Her eyes were shining. She remembered all of them, all of her old students over the years. We looked at the pictures and they scared us, because all of those children were grown up now. They had to be the ages of our babysitters or even older. We thought they looked funny. The boys had duck tails or brush cuts. A few boys in my class still had brush cuts but they were dying out, styles were changing. The times were changing too, we were still having air-raid drills in the school basement but they didn't really scare us, we thought it was fun to go down there and pretend that someday we'd have to use up all the canned food stored down there. Anyway, it was Christmas of 1964 or 1965, I was just ten or eleven and just beginning to have a sense of what year it was and what it meant. I remember thinking there was something wrong with those pictures of all those children who were not like me and Miss Bells saying how wonderful they all were. She didn't think anything was wrong with them, in fact I got the feeling she liked them better than us, those children in those years, 1952, 1953, 1954, all through the fifties. She put a year to each picture, all those years I couldn't remember because I was too young or I wasn't even born. I remember blaming the strangeness of the children in the photographs on the fact that they lived in those strange years. I wonder if Miss Bells had showed them their class pictures ten years later, if those kids would have gotten the creeps about those years of their

125

childhood or if they would have thought they all looked perfectly ordinary. Because now when I look back on the years of my childhood I get the creeps, I remember a lot of murders, but in those days even though I knew about the murders they didn't seem like anything out of the ordinary. In Miss Bells's class that day I just thought it was the fifties that were wrong. Because Miss Bells took one last photograph and showed it to the class and said, One boy in this picture went bad.

4

The young woman asked Bobby if he'd been shown the photo of the boy who went bad too. Bobby reminded her that he had left the school in the mid-fifties. He had already told her that but somehow, looking at the youthful and modern-looking man in his mid-thirties having coffee in her kitchen, she had forgotten.

Oh yeah, the young woman said. I wish I could remember what year the picture of the boy who went bad belonged to. Maybe he was in your class.

Maybe he was, agreed Bobby.

Maybe Miss Bells didn't tell us what year that photo was, the young woman said. I do remember she wouldn't tell us the boy's name and she wouldn't even point out his face. That was what made it so scary. It might have been any of them. All of them looked wrong to me, but to Miss Bells all of them looked right and only one went wrong. And for some reason she wouldn't tell us which one, she wanted to protect him, even though he wasn't innocent anymore.

It might have been me, Bobby said. He couldn't resist admitting it. Having confessed, he gave up the idea of someday robbing the young woman's house. His heart went out to Miss Bells, the same kind of surging feeling he'd had when he'd met that other music teacher, his wife, who had known nothing about him. Miss Bells had been an old maid but she hadn't been as stupid as the rest: she knew he was bad. But she had been forgiving, because he had had such an angelic voice—an accident, since he hated music. Miss Bells had been heartbroken when he gave up the Glee Club for the Woods Gang, and worse. And if, ten years after the fact, she was still talking about him, still showing his picture around, it meant she'd never gotten over him, even though she knew he had become a thief.

Oh, I doubt it, the young woman said to Bobby. Miss Bells didn't say what the boy did to go bad but I think it might have been murder.

Hell, Bobby said. I might have been a JD in those days but I wasn't a murderer.

That's right, the young woman said. That came later, in the sixties. Did Miss Bells wear pancake makeup back then? In the fifties?

Yes, Bobby said, though he wasn't sure what pancake makeup was. She probably still looks exactly the same, the young woman said, those rhinestone glasses are still probably hanging down her throat. She and Bobby started laughing like old pals, like fellow-students in Miss Bells's music class, in a time that never was. Not for a moment did the young woman dream that she might indeed be killing time with the boy who went bad. She pictured Bobby as the babysitter's boyfriend, a teenage rebel, even though by the days of the babysitter Bobby was a young man, old enough to be one of the mid-sixties murderers. She thought of her little girl, how lucky she was to be growing up safe. Bobby, in danger of falling in love again, told the young woman she had missed nothing in the fifties, their crimes were overrated. The boy who went bad, he said, probably just stole a few hubcaps. For the moment he forgot the murder Miss Bells knew nothing about.

Dominica

DOMINICA, a dominatrix, tells near-strangers quite frankly that she "beats men for a living." Also, that her real name is Nancy. As a rule Dominica does not like to divulge much else about her work, though she claims to have a private life as good as anyone's.

By "good," Dominica means virtuous. . . . When she leaves her dungeon for the day she has no second thoughts. She calls her mother frequently, she gives her old clothes to the Goodwill, and when her friends tell jokes that aren't funny she laughs at them dutifully. In the beginning she found her job quite funny, and used to tell stories of her own after work, but then, several years ago, an accident happened, and Dominica stopped talking. In a turnabout, she decided to take her work quite seriously—not while she was doing it, but afterwards, in her leisure time. For several months she meticulously recorded everything her subjects said about themselves, or screamed, or whimpered, thinking that in these catalogues she might find out something important about human nature. Except for the fact that some men like to be beaten, she didn't. But this cheered her up. And now she gives her job no second thoughts at all . . . preferring to think about the island she named herself after, Dominica, her plans to visit it someday, and the acquisition of a secret wardrobe of bright suitable things.

At three in the morning, one morning, Dominica returns to the apartment she shares with her boyfriend, a painter. In relation to painters—and Dominica has had a long string of painter-boyfriends—Dominica sees herself as a capable, pragmatic businesswoman. But she also likes a little beauty in her life. Her current painter, Dietrich, paints crudely but colorfully, and he is also known as the most beautiful boy in the city. He doesn't mind what she does. Dietrich is a romantic type, lost in the clouds and the bottle. He thinks Dominica is pretty and sweet and wicked, all at the same time, and it excites him. When Dominica returns home at three in the morning, her day done, Dietrich is also just coming home—from a nightclub, usually—and they have normal sex. And then they sleep together and when they wake up he paints and she fixes him drinks, until in the early evening she goes off to work. When Dominica gets home at three in the morning, one morning, it is just like every other weeknight as far as Dietrich is concerned. He likes this domestic life. He calls Dominica Nancy.

Another night, though, Nancy does not come home. She is instead in a dark bedroom suburb, drinking coffee at the kitchen table with her mother. Nancy's mother is upset about the neighbors—more than upset, frightened—and Nancy has agreed to stay the night to comfort and protect her mother. They are both wearing bathrobes that belong to Nancy's mother and Nancy feels comfortable but not dangerous enough to scare off the neighbors. Nancy's mother thinks the neighbors are dangerous because one of them, a girl, screams night and day, and the dogs bark night and day, and none of them stop when somebody suggests they do. Nancy's mother suggested it—very politely—when she found herself face-to-face with the mad daughter that day in the alley, and the girl swore violently at her. Now Nancy's mother thinks the family is out to get her. "Everyone says they're in the Mafia," she whispers. She can't stop telling Nancy about the mad daughter's eyes, mad tortured eyes. According to the Mafia family's father, the girl suffered a drug over-dose and fell into a coma lasting several years, from which she recently awakened, screaming. Nancy's mother does not think this is possible. "Is it?" she asks Nancy, know-ing that her daughter too has a past, but thankful that Nancy's eyes are still so blue and serene.

Dominica is too pragmatic to invent another past for herself, preferring to think instead about her future on a bright island. . . . But sometimes she has odd dreams. In them she is Nancy, leaning against a dark doorway, wor-rying about whether or not she looks seductive enough to make a living. And then she is suddenly underneath a strange man in a dark room, suffering. . . . She wakes up grateful that she has turned things around, that she is no longer an ordinary prostitute. Until the dream fades Do-minica basks in the warmth of a past that explains every-thing.

Dietrich is worried about Nancy's tax return—how will she explain what they live on?—and asks her if she knows a man at the IRS. Nancy says yes, he comes to me every Tuesday, and will do anything I say. Good, says Dietrich, command him to overlook you. As far as he's concerned you don't exist. Do you think you have that power?

Dietrich has this dream often and wakes up with a feel-ing of great pleasure, though Nancy fades away before she can answer.

Usually, of course, Nancy's body is next to his in bed,

sleeping like an angel. When Dietrich wakes up alone this particular morning, he begins to worry. It is inevitable, he thinks, that someday some man Nancy is beating will forget himself. . . .

But Nancy is still at her mother's, having coffee in the kitchen. Her mother is still worrying about the neighbors, but she is afraid to bore Nancy by going on and on. In the clear light of day and her mother's silence Nancy has forgotten all about the threat of the neighbors, but she is worried about the time. Dietrich can wait (she likes the idea of Dietrich worrying about her safety), but she has to leave her mother's place soon, or else she might run into Mr. D.—and it would do no good to let him see her in a bathrobe, with her mother, talking in the kitchen.

Nancy's mother is not very domestic, but her kitchen is spotlessly clean. This is because (as she admits quite frankly) Mr. Dee, a friend of Nancy's, comes in every other day at lunchtime to clean it. Mr. Dee is a big man of about fifty, an important business executive. Housekeeping is his hobby. It puzzled Nancy's mother, at first—not that Mr. Dee liked to clean house, but that he never seemed to worry about getting his three-piece suit dirty. Since Mr. Dee went about his cleaning with great dignity and reserve—he barely spoke a word, and worked too efficiently to be drawn into idle chitchat—Nancy's mother was afraid to suggest that perhaps he might invest some of his vast fortune in an outfit more suitable for his hobby. One day she got up her courage. "After all, Mr. Dee," she said, "gardeners wear gloves, joggers wear sweatpants. . . ." Mr. Dee looked embarrassed and explained rather quietly that he only felt comfortable in a suit. Nancy's mother begged his pardon.

For a moment Mr. D. forgot himself. He told her about his office—about his private washroom, his closets full of suits and shirts, and the secretary he orders to take them to the cleaners.

After leaving her mother's, Dominica stops in at a fashionable hair salon to visit Eloise, an old friend.

Eloise used to be a dominatrix. Several of Dominica's old colleagues have become hairdressers, but Eloise is one of the most successful, perhaps because when she was a dominatrix she was known as Delilah. When she changed professions, she went back to calling herself Eloise—it wasn't good business to scare away patrons right off the bat. Eloise scares them later. She has a reputation for bullying her clients into submitting to haircuts that make them look nothing like what they had imagined. She turns glamour girls into little boys, merely by chopping all their hair off. These days Eloise also gets glamourous young men in her salon. They already have short hair, so Eloise turns them into fruits: she sculpts the backs of heads in the shape and texture of pineapples, and exposes naked brows as wide as melons.

Eloise makes heads look like pineapples and melons because she too dreams of a sunny tropical island— unspecified.

When Dominica arrives, Eloise quickly clips off a few more inches from the head she is working on, goes to the sink, and furiously washes the hair off her hands.

Despite all the hair on the floor, Eloise's salon is a nice clean establishment. The light is bright through the windows and potted plants sit on the sills. Pleasant synthesizer music plays somewhere in the background, and the severe-looking young woman sitting in the chair seems happy with her haircut. But Eloise does not look happy.

Let's take a vacation, suggests Dominica.

The last time Dominica seriously made vacation plans was several years ago, when the accident happened. She was working with a partner named Lulu then, a girl nobody could take seriously as a dominatrix because she had a funny name. But Lulu, as it happened, took her work very seriously. . . . Her boyfriend, who was supposed to protect them, suggested that Lulu and Dominica take a vacation until the matter was cleared up. Dominica invested in dollar-wise guides to the Caribbean. It was then that she discovered she was not, after all, the namesake of the Dominican Republic, a land with a bloody and dangerous past. There was another Dominica—Do-mi-neek-a, an island of lush tropical jungles to get lost in. Lulu was not a nature girl and wanted to go to Bermuda, but when she heard that Dominica was the last reservation of the Carib Indians, former cannibals, she capitulated. They left the apartment and the accident for somebody else to discover.

A few days later Nancy read in the newspaper about a strange smell in a fashionable townhouse, and the subsequent discovery of its source in a locked closet. She was staying at her mother's house, in the suburbs but still in town, because out of the blue a hurricane, David, had hit Dominica and destroyed it. It was some weeks before it was safe for Dominica to go back to work. Lulu's boyfriend set her up in a new location, alone (Lulu had gone to Bermuda, after all, and never came back), but he didn't think it was necessary for her to change her name. It had all been Lulu's fault anyway, Dominica had been in another room with another man at the time, and she hadn't ever killed anybody. And she still hasn't. For the most part Dominica has kept the horror of that night buried in some dark place, and she supposes that that's where the corpse is buried too.

Dominica is back to normal, Nancy tells Dietrich, so that's where we're going. She doesn't invite him or even ask his opinion. Dietrich is hurt. Why all of a sudden do you want to go on vacation with Eloise? he asks. I felt sorry for her, Nancy replies, she looked like she needed a vacation.

But what about me? Dietrich wants to know. I won't be gone long, Nancy promises him. You'll be all right. I'll drink myself to death, Dietrich says darkly, and then they both laugh, because no matter how happy Nancy makes him she can never make him stop drinking anyway.

Nancy's mother thinks Dietrich is a drunkard and she is not at all sorry that Nancy is going on vacation with a girl friend instead. But she wishes out loud that Nancy was not going away at all, for who will protect her when the neighbors start screaming and barking again and come to get her? It's been quiet lately, her mother admits, but only because the father of the house, the one who is supposed to be in the Mafia, is home, and when he's home everybody is afraid of him and shuts up. But the father of the house only visits every other weekend, and the rumor is that the rest of the time he spends with his mistress and a second, secret family. "He must be a dangerous man," Nancy's mother says, "but I can't help feeling sorry for him, with that crazy daughter and those mad dogs, and did I tell you that one of the two sons is vicious? He tortures the dogs, maybe that's why they bark so much."

"We could get you a dog," Nancy suggests, "a guard-dog to protect you. A vicious one."

"No," her mother says, "I don't like dogs, and you can never tell with vicious ones, they can turn on you. What I really need is a man in the house."

"Dietrich could come and stay with you," Nancy says, but her mother snorts with laughter at the idea that a drunk like Dietrich could ever protect her.

Soon after receiving the news of her daughter's impending vacation, Nancy's mother goes to her kitchen window and looks out into the alley. In the shadows she sees a tall, dark figure, a big and strong man carrying a bag. It must be Father, she thinks, leaving his crazy family. I can't blame him for getting away and getting his pleasure elsewhere. It's too bad, though, because what that family really needs is a man in the house.

As Father emerges from the shadows, Nancy's mother is surprised to discover that it is really Mr. Dee, carrying his briefcase full of cleaning supplies, making his way to her front door.

She hurries to the bathroom and has just enough time to comb her hair and put on lipstick before the doorbell rings.

Dietrich is hurt. He had been in the bedroom, listening in on the extension to the conversation between Nancy and her mother, and he is still smarting from Nancy's mother's derisive laughter. When Nancy gets off the phone he storms into the kitchen. How dare your mother think I'm not good enough for you, he screams, just because I'm an artist.

But Nancy is preoccupied. She is wondering who to get to protect her mother while she is on vacation. Of course there were always Lulu's ex-boyfriend's men, but they might very well know the dangerous neighbors, so Nancy cannot risk it.

If your mother knew what you really do for a living it would kill her, adds Dietrich. Someday she'll find out the truth, and then we'll see who has the last laugh.

It's not funny, says Nancy sharply, but anyway after all these years she hasn't suspected a thing, I've made sure of that. What makes you think she'll find out now?

Somebody could tell her the truth, Dietrich says darkly, somebody who's not afraid of you.

Nancy knows this is just an idle threat and is about to tell Dietrich to shut up when the phone rings. Surprisingly, it is her mother again.

"What about Mr. Dee?" her mother whispers. "It's his day off, but he came over to clean the house anyway, that's how I got the idea. He's big and strong and he'd do anything for you. Could you ask him to come and be my bodyguard?"

There is nothing else Dominica can do. She thinks of the many times, before sending him off to clean house, she'd made Mr. D. cower in a corner, but she has to give in to her mother.

He's hardly a normal man, she tells a disinterested Dietrich later, normally he couldn't protect a fly. But I can fix that. I'll order him to be dangerous.

Eloise and Dominica go on a shopping trip. Eloise buys three bikinis, but Dominica buys only one, since she has two bikinis (plus matching cover-ups) hidden in her closet, a few years out of style perhaps, but still bright and beautiful. . . .

It'll be good for you to get out of black rubber for a change, Eloise jokes, waving a white rubber bathing cap, and Dominica laughs.

At the dungeon she is so good-natured that some of her clients complain. And now that her island is no longer a dream, at night she falls into a dreamless sleep.

Dietrich, sleeping beside her, has a recurring dream that he is an IRS agent. He tracks Nancy down to Dominica, arrests her, chains her, and puts her in prison, a dark place surrounded by a moat so deep and wide she cannot swim away, and nobody can hear her screams.

When Mr. Dee arrives at six every evening, Nancy's mother has his dinner waiting for him. She has taken a new interest in domestic matters since Mr. Dee has become her bodyguard instead of her housekeeper. It was Nancy's mother's idea to cook him dinner, and since she found she enjoyed it, she offered to do the cleaning as well. Mr. Dee seemed reluctant, at first, to give up his hobby, but Nancy's mother insisted that an important man must have more important things to do with his lunch hour than clean her house. "You're quite right," said Mr. Dee.

After dinner Mr. Dee goes to the window and looks out into the alley to see what the neighbors are up to. At first Nancy's mother, afraid of disturbing him, stayed in the kitchen, but one day she got up her courage and went to the window and joined him. He didn't seem to mind. For several days they watched the alley together in silence. There was nothing much to see in the alley, though, and the neighbors were being unusually quiet; Father must be in the house, Nancy's mother decided. In her own house Mr. Dee's uncommunicative silence began to weigh on her. She knew Mr. Dee did not like to talk much, Nancy had warned her of that, but it couldn't hurt to talk to him. . . . And now their evenings are quite lively. Mr. Dee still does not talk much, but he is a good listener, and occasionally he asks her to get him a drink or something to eat. It is almost as if they were married, Nancy's mother thinks, forgetting herself.

Then one day she gets a postcard from Nancy in Dominica, and remembers that although Mr. Dee is old enough to be Nancy's father, it is Nancy that he is crazy about. Maybe it would be a good thing. Nancy could leave Dietrich and her miserable job as a night waitress and settle down with Mr. Dee. Suddenly Nancy's mother feels a bit guilty; she has told Mr. Dee everything about herself, but she has forgotten to mention Nancy. Dutifully she shows him Nancy's postcard. "She's a long way away, isn't she?" says Mr. Dee, rather nastily.

"Has she hurt your feelings by going away?" Nancy's mother whispers. "But she's really a very sweet girl." She begins to recount Nancy's virtues.

In Dominica, Nancy and Eloise have a wonderful time. During the mornings they wear their bikinis and lounge by the pool at the hotel, and in the afternoons they explore the island's wilderness. Unlike Lulu, Eloise is a nature girl at heart. Their favorite places are Boiling Lake and Sulphur Springs, reminders of the island's volcanic past. Nancy half-expects that something terrible will happen—not a hurricane this time, but maybe a volcano. In her guidebook she'd read that "some Dominicans fear that volcanic activity will erupt again." In the evenings there are no nightclubs to go to, so Eloise gives her lessons on how to cut hair. In her suitcase Eloise has several heads of hair—wigs she'd brought from home—to practice on. Nancy enjoys cutting hair. How could you have been so unhappy at the salon? she asks Eloise. I was just overworked, Eloise says.

Before they leave Dominica, Nancy decides to become a hairdresser and Eloise's partner in the salon. There is no real reason now for her to change careers, but she thinks it might be fun to lead a normal life, and she could cut her mother's hair for free.

No volcano erupts. The future looks serene. But when Nancy returns from Dominica, she discovers that Mr. D. has killed her mother.

I told you it would kill her, says Dietrich with a laugh.

But in a week Nancy has convinced her mother that she has put her past behind her, and things return to normal.

Our Perfect Partners

"KEN GRABBER! Oh, that guy's a nymphomaniac," he said disparagingly. I had never heard a man described as a nymphomaniac before. But semantics could wait. I wanted to know more details. The women he had rushed into bed with, and why. But all Guy could tell me was that Ken Grabber thought about women day and night, and talked about them a good deal too. In fact during any conversation—whether about law or otherwise, for Ken and Guy are both lawyers—Ken Grabber would see fit to introduce the subject of women. Women he had dated and who would not, for the most part, sleep with him. "Oh," I said, "then it doesn't sound as if he really is a nymphomaniac after all." Nymphomaniacs get their man, or in this case, their woman. "And anyway," I corrected Guy, "men can't be nymphomaniacs."

Although oversexed Southerners are not my type, I was secretly disappointed that Ken Grabber had not, so to speak, made a grab for me. But that's a cheap joke. His name is not Grabber any more than mine is. Something completely different. Something that shall remain secret.

The law is an open book, but the workings of a law firm are usually secretive. Prospective employees have to sign a release, before they are hired. A release like a promise, a promise of fidelity and obedience. No private gain to be had from privy knowledge, and so forth. At the root of it all is money, I guess, but from money and its concerns, morality is made. The secret reason that in our law firm (as in all law firms) liaisons between lawyers and non-lawyers are frowned upon (if not actually outlawed) is that the partners are afraid that some financial secret might be spilled upon the pillow during . . . pillow talk.

Ken Grabber has not, to my knowledge, made a play for any of the non-legal (as they call us, as if we were criminal) personnel at the firm; but he has, reportedly, made certain off-color remarks to a young female lawyer—a good-looker, but a stuffy one, just another in a line of Ken Grabber's non-conquests.

Meanwhile, unbeknownst to most, most certainly to his six children, Mickey Plotnick, boy-wonder partner, trafficker in movie-company deals, lives a secret life. . . .

Sidney, my partner—not a partner in the law firm, but my proofreading partner—dreams of proofreading food. Not surprising, since he likes to eat. In one of his former jobs, he claims, a secret room was filled to the ceiling with Pepperidge Farm cookies. Cookies of all descriptions and nationalities, all produced by Pepperidge Farm, which was this law firm's client. In this Pepperidge Farm paradise Sidney gained ten pounds. But Sidney did not get sweeter. That process is reserved for the coming of maturity, or a really neat blonde girlfriend.

No love is lost between Sidney and the lawyers. Hatred is too strong a word to use. There is just no love lost, no love to be wasted. Everybody minds his own business. Mickey Plotnick, for example, does not waste his time greeting Sidney, nor has he ever so much as inclined his head in greeting to me, though we have passed each other in the halls for a year and a half. In his small hooded eyes I have sometimes detected a gleam of recognition, but perhaps I am mistaken. . . . In any case it is not a benevolent gleam. But Mickey must love somebody, he must love his kids, or why else would he let them run wild in the halls of our office? They are a nuisance to everybody, but Mickey Plotnick loves them.

Mickey Plotnick's office is cluttered with photographs of his six kids. He is a little man, always on the go. You have to be on the go to be in the movie business, however marginally. Mickey Plotnick is only in it marginally; he has something to do with a bank that finances motion pictures, and most of them are not even major—a lot of them are horror flicks. (Production was held up on one movie because the producers could not obtain enough bats.) Nevertheless Mickey Plotnick reaps certain rewards; he gets a lot of tickets to screenings. If the movies are innocent enough, and not too horrific, he lets his six kids come along. Does he ever think that the halls of our office are not innocent enough for his kids to frolic in? Of course not. Ken Grabber sits on another floor, and besides, he is not interested in children.

Sidney likes to reminisce about the law firms he used to work at; he is particularly fond of the place where all the word processors were fat, save one. You would think Sidney might have liked the non-fat one, but no. Sidney likes a certain amount of heft on his women, perhaps so they will not criticize the heft on Sidney. Otherwise, though, he wants a woman who is exactly not like his mother; he wants a Protestant with blonde hair who will find Sidney exotic enough to go to bed with.

Has Ken Grabber gone to bed with Mickey Plotnick's wife? Is Mickey's secret life that of cuckold? That is impossible, just as it is impossible (technically) for Ken Grabber to be a nymphomaniac. *Mickey Plotnick lives a secret life.* That is the premise. That requires an active plot, or at least an active imagination. To be cuckolded is hardly a way of life; it is not a lifestyle, it is nothing to be lived or not lived; it is just a passive state, a non-event, like Ken Grabber's seductions, which do not take place.

Mergers, takeovers, ship bankruptcies: these are the dramas of the law office, maybe not the stuff of life or gossip, but still pretty interesting, to those who know what the secrets are. . . . On the high seas several ships were seized by their creditors. The lawyers searched far and wide to get those ships for their clients. They traveled to distant countries, lay low in foreign ports. In the dead of night they stole aboard the ships while the sailors were sleeping. Sleeping innocently. . . . Or sleeping with each other?

There is a secret relation between Ed, the supply-room clerk, and Vladimir, the messenger. Of course Ed and Vladimir are not their real names. Would I besmirch the reputations of these young men by my off-color remarks? Yes, but I would not use their real names.

Vladimir is called Vladimir because I believe he, or his recent ancestors, came from a Slavic country. I once heard him speaking a foreign tongue. He is a young man with a bad complexion, but he has his youth, which is saying something, because he works with messengers who have lost their youth, their health, their dignity, and some- times their sense. One messenger shakes, another loses his way and ends up in Boston when he is supposed to be in Philadelphia. Or is this the same messenger? Vladimir, on the other hand, has a sardonic sense of humor and a facility at two languages, English and whatever the other one is. It is even possible that given these natural advan- tages he earns a better salary than the other messengers, who are out of the running of life but may have made a good living in the past; Sidney thinks at least three of them may once have owned delis.

And Ed, what about him? Ed is called Ed because he reminds the casual observer of Mr. Ed, the talking horse.

He is long and lean, and he leans his long head (a Slavic head) out of the corral, or rather over the demi-door of the supply room. Ed has a sense of humor. He doesn't mind when I walk by humming "A horse is a horse." He also has two kids and a wife, and he is just twenty-two, and he only makes about ten thousand dollars a year, if that much.

But Mr. Ed has just walked off his job. He is no longer with us. And that is how I found out about the secret relation between Ed and Vladimir. Ed is gone but not dead, and I know that because somebody told me that Ed has been seen, alive and well, in Vladimir's apartment building. He's been seen there because he lives there, and he lives there because Vladimir is his brother-in-law, something I never knew until Ed was gone and buried, or rather out to pasture, but if you look in the company phone book you can see the truth, or part of it—no mention of their being brothers-in-law, but they do indeed live at the same number on the same street in the same city. Jersey City, New Jersey.

Ken Grabber will soon be going South to see his family; he is soon to attend his cousin's wedding. What makes Ken dread this normally happy event is that his cousin's wedding happens to be the same day as his fortieth birthday, and he is afraid that all his old aunts will question him about his bachelor status. Ken Grabber perhaps suspects his old aunts of evil thoughts. Little do they know of all the women he has bedded, or at least desired to bed; so perhaps they think he is a bachelor because he prefers the company of men. In some sense they are right. Ken Grabber does not seem very comfortable in the company of women. He is a jokester; one of the secretaries at the firm thinks he is "corny," although Ken no doubt thinks he is a great wit. I can imagine Ken Grabber on a date: he makes jokes all through dinner, he won't shut up during the movie, afterwards he has too much to drink and grabs a knee to test the waters; and then when the evening winds to a close he tries to disarm his date into going to bed with him. He makes a lot of corny/witty jokes and says absurd things just to see where it will lead him, even though he knows quite well where it will lead; by this time his date thinks he is a drunk, silly little boy, not at all suitable for marriage, which is a shame since he earns a decent salary. I could explain all this to Ken Grabber's aunts, but I have not been invited to the wedding—Ken Grabber has not even invited me out for dinner.

Now Ken has left the firm, and so has Guy. They are leaving in droves. Both Ken and Guy plan to do "creative projects"—Ken, for example, wants to take pictures. Guy is going to write books—a common lawyer's secret desire. But not all lawyers actually leave to write them. And if they do leave, the lawyers do not generally leave under a cloud like Mr. Ed did, or like one of our old messengers did, a few months ago, when he disappeared on his way to the bank with $7,000 of company money. It was his job to deposit that money. I presumed the poor old guy dead too until somebody told me he'd been discovered in Las Vegas, gambling the last of his life away and losing it all, the money anyway. He came back to New York and turned himself in. No longer does he live the life of a gambler; it has been decided that he must pay back (to the partners) every last cent of the money he first stole, then lost, even if it takes him the rest of his life, even if the rest of his life isn't long enough. One wonders what will become of his meager estate; will his grandchildren be plunged into debt? But that is a question for our trusts-and-estates department, and of course our ex-messenger could never afford their services, which is a shame, since he will probably die soon and in debt. Guy, on the other hand, has at least thirty good years to go, and he gave a month's notice to the firm, and so everything is, for him, correct and on schedule. The only mystery is, why did our messenger leave for Las Vegas when he had $7,000 in his pocket, and not $20,000, as he'd had in his pocket the week before?

Was it art, or money, or girl trouble, that caused Guy to leave the law firm for greener pastures? But no, the pastures belong to Mr. Ed, not Guy. Guy is now (from nine to five; in the evening he is devoted to his new word processor) in the happy world of advertising. His job is to decide whether or not the ads that the creative people in the agency create will get anybody into trouble. Since Guy never gets into any trouble himself, but wishes he would, this job is a dream come true. Now he can look for trouble, for off-color remarks, under the cover of a respectable well-paying job. Off-color remarks are sometimes okay, of course, in this advertising age, as long as you don't cast untruthful aspersions on your competitors, your rivals. . . . It is totally untruthful of me to cast aspersions on Mickey Plotnick's wife, who is almost certainly not unfaithful, who hardly exists so far except as the mother of his six children, and who would probably have little time to cuckold Mickey even if she wanted to. (Even *when* she wanted to.) Six children are a handful, especially these particular children. When they are not running around the halls of our office—and to be truthful, that only occurs a few times a year, during school holidays—they must be running around the halls of school, and the halls of the Plotnick house. They must be running rings around Mickey Plotnick's wife. It is not surprising that she looks at Mickey and doesn't really see him, that she is blind to Mickey's secret life.

A secret life demands a plot; but it is going to take a convoluted plot to get Mickey, Guy, Ken, Ed and

147

Vladimir, and Sidney in the same room. It is true that they have all walked the halls of the same building, day after day, but a building is a big place. Our law firm occupies three floors, and even though all but Ken Grabber have worked on the same floor (an amazing coincidence; less amazing when you know that it is also my floor), nobody knows anybody else. Except Ed and Vladimir, of course, who are related by marriage, and Ken and Guy, who are more or less on the same level, if not the same floor (though it seems Guy's knowledge of Ken consists only of his reputation for nymphomania).

Otherwise, it is remarkable how little any of these people have to do with each other. Guy does not remember Ed or Vladimir at all, and though he laughed long and hard at the description of Mickey (and Mickey's annoying kids), he has never worked with Mickey; it is all just a superficial impression. Ed and Vladimir have no doubt heard of Guy, Ken, and Mickey, but in their roles as supply-clerk and messenger, respectively, they have kept their respectful distance. And Mickey, for his part, as partner, is certain to have no clear idea who anybody is. (Not every partner is so undemocratic; one charming old gentleman, who resembles Fred Astaire, tips his hat—so to speak—to all who cross his path.) Of course, Guy, Mr. Ed, and Ken Grabber have all since left the premises, and in their cases Mickey has an excuse—out of sight, out of mind. But there is still Vladimir, and as far as Vladimir goes—well, from all appearances, Vladimir does not exist as far as Mickey is concerned. He is there but not noticed, like the furniture, or the proofreaders, or the pictures of old whaling ships. Get me a messenger! Mickey might command Theresa, his sullen Irish secretary; and it is all the same to Mickey Plotnick whether the messenger is the young wisecracking Vladimir, or one of the old ex-deli-owners.

Still, Mickey is smart; you don't get to be a boy-

148

wonder partner if you're not smart, and maybe Mickey
has heard the story of the messenger who ended up in the
wrong city; Mickey would not like to entrust his important movie-deal documents to this messenger. If he were
smart he would recognize Vladimir and value him for his
youth, wit, and energy. But if he were smart would he let
his esteem for Vladimir show? Mickey is no Fred Astaire;
he does not have the credentials to be charming in that
old-fashioned noblesse-oblige way. To impress his elders
Mickey has to be a mogul—not a movie mogul, but a
legal beagle, sharp and ruthless. He has to make them a
lot of money, to prove the gamble they took on him was
worth it. He does not want to spend the rest of his life
paying them back (like the old messenger has to); a few
more years, a few more dollars should do it. Then maybe
Mickey will relax enough to reveal his secret. It might be
anything his fellow-partners would disapprove of: liaisons
with Vladimir, or with Ed, or with Vladimir and Ed and
Ed's wife, who is Vladimir's sister; or just with Vladimir's
sister, who is Slavic too. Or perhaps the secret is only that
Mickey is related, by blood or marriage, to one or more of
the old messengers; maybe all of the ex-deli-owners are
his uncles. . . .

Whatever Mickey's secret is, Theresa has nothing to do
with it. Nobody, in my wildest imagination, could bark
out "Theresa!" to his mistress, and no mistress would
ever answer back "What?" with such a marked lack of
interest. Theresa, Mickey Plotnick's sullen but efficient
Irish secretary, does tease him sometimes, she even talks
back to him, but she always calls him Mr. Plotnick; she
doesn't dare call him Mickey. Theresa strikes me as a girl
with no future. I wonder about her sometimes, but not
too much.

Theresa, to my knowledge, is unmarried, but she would
never consider dating Sidney, Ken, or Guy, those three

bachelors on the loose. Sidney is too eccentric, Ken too corny, Guy too broken-hearted. And anyway Theresa's taste probably runs to cops. That is no doubt unfair of me, but since I hardly know Theresa (she is as sullen to me as she is to Mickey), I cannot resist putting her in a category. From all appearances, however, Theresa does not seem to be the perfect partner for any of the bachelors. Sidney would find her blonde enough, and even though she is Catholic he would forgive her (he seems to think only Protestants are cool enough to balance his mania); but in the end Theresa is not Sidney's type any more than Sidney is Theresa's. She would not appreciate Sidney's wit and artistry, at the way he can magically transform himself (during a dull session proofreading a revolving credit agreement) into a canasta-playing matriarch who has decided to leave her husband and her meat loaf and rejoin the working world. Nor could she appreciate Ken Grabber's wit, which revolves around the world of popular music and popular electronics; Theresa likes to discuss pets and needlepoint. Does this make her a perfect partner for a cop? Not at all, no more than it makes her an ideal date for Guy, who, though dull, would secretly think Theresa much duller. He wouldn't take her to a jazz club or out to dinner, but he might put her into his next mystery novel, if it is a police procedural—perhaps as a cop's wife.

Mickey, Ed, Vladimir, et al. . . . Why does Mickey always come first? Is it because his private life (unlike Ed's, or Vladimir's, or Guy's, or Ken's, or Sidney's) is as yet unrevealed, ripe with possibilities, rife with danger and mystery? Is it because Mickey is a partner of the firm and therefore entitled to our respect? Or is it because, speculation about his messenger-uncles notwithstanding, Mickey has no relation to anybody in the office? Sidney, Guy, and Ken Grabber are the three searching bachelors; Ed and

Vladimir are brothers-in-law; but Mickey is a loner. None of the other partners are Micky's pal. Is that because none of them do movie deals, or because Mickey is just too rude? What the other partners think of Mickey is secret; but the bottom line is that Mickey has nobody to chat with at the office, except Theresa, and Mickey can only talk to her in the most mechanical, artificial way. Get me this, get me that, Theresa; it is no wonder that Theresa is sullen. Is he so commanding with his wife? It is hard to imagine Mickey outside the office; he might be a much better person, or he might be much worse. It's a shame that Mrs. Plotnick is not more visible; I have never seen her on the premises of the law firm, ever. I've seen the children, of course, those six pretty brats, but although they do have Mickey's energy, they don't look anything like him. Mickey does have connections in the movie business; maybe he hires child actors to run around at holiday-time, pretending to be his, so that nobody will suspect what a horror Mickey Plotnick really is.

Everybody knows what Ken Grabber is; he is a nymphomaniac, even though technically male nymphomaniacs do not exist. In Guy's imagination (an ordinary-guy imagination) Ken Grabber is a nymphomaniac, and that is the important thing, to Guy at least. But it is also important to know that Guy has a crush on that goodlooking stuffy female lawyer Ken once unwisely made a pass at. To punish Ken Grabber, Guy spread the news far and wide of Ken Grabber's nymphomania, and like most at the law firm I believed the worst; but for some reason the rumor remained a secret to Ken Grabber for quite a while. Maybe nobody at the firm talks to Ken Grabber much. But one night I talked too much. Ken and I accidentally found ourselves at the same non-company party; when I ambled up to him and destroyed his in-progress seduction in an instant ("I hear you're a nymphomaniac, Ken," I said genially), Ken was both surprised and hurt. It was then that I realized that never should you always believe everything you hear.

Ken Grabber was, in fact, so disgruntled with me for destroying his reputation, his pride, and his would-be seduction, that now he will never ask me to dinner. I know this with certainty; nevertheless, the other night I could not help dreaming about him. We were going out to dinner, and despite my fears Ken refrained from making corny jokes; he was a perfectly charming and delightful dinner companion. After dinner, we took in a movie, and though in the dark I rather wished Ken would steal his arm around my shoulder, schoolboy-style, he didn't; he was a perfect gentleman. Nor did he, during the movie, chatter away; he was so silent I was not the least distracted from my dreams. After the movie, we had a cappuccino in a quaint café (something I had never imagined Ken Grabber doing—another surprise); and then he was about to put me in a cab, when I surprised myself by inviting myself to his apartment—which was, conveniently, located nearby. Ken graciously acquiesced. His apartment was furnished with none of the standard accoutrements of the desperate bachelor; it was instead a tasteful, if somewhat bland, setting, a testimony to Ken's mild and gallant temperament. The man would surely someday make partner. . . . But perhaps that was the foreshadowing of the horror to come. As Ken finally, passionately stole his arm around me (we were sitting on a sofa which might at any moment become a sofa bed), and muffled his mouth into the folds of my neck, I screamed. Ken had disappeared! Or—if I really looked at who was biting my neck—he had suddenly turned into Mickey Plotnick—

But Mickey is not the perfect partner; he is hardly typical. Except for Mickey Plotnick, who is known as one sharp lawyer, and illustrates this with energy and volubility (too much volubility, is the secret opinion of many), our lawyers quietly go about their business. Their progress down our carpeted halls is almost somnambulistic. They are ostensibly in search of something, a document from word-processing or a cup of coffee or a partner, but at all times they are all business. In their hands they carry sheaves of papers, and their eyes study the ceiling, the baseboards, or (in those areas our visitors are most likely to see) our expensive Oriental rugs. (My own office is bare, spare, utilitarian, and hidden in a corner; that is its charm.) Everything else is invisible. The tradition for this well-bred reticence goes back to the nineteenth century, as does our law firm. Along with our pictures of whaling ships, and maps of Olde New York before the firm existed, we have several memorials to well-bred, reticent, well-paid men. On the wall opposite my out-of-the-way office, for example, hangs a row of portraits of famous men. I believe they are all former Supreme Court justices, although one of them is also a former President. It is possible, but not probable, that these dead men were also once exemplary members of the firm.

Since Ken Grabber and Guy have both left us before they became partners, their pictures will never grace the firm's walls; in due time they will be forgotten. But neither of them loses any sleep over this. They plan to become famous, which will insure their immortality (in any case their pictures will appear in the newspaper). In the meantime they might practice a little law, here and there, but . . . it's not as if the law is in their blood. . . .

The law is in Mickey Plotnick's blood, but so are the movies. Is that why Mickey is the way he is, does he live in a dream world? . . . When Mickey was a kid he used to go to matinees; he skipped school and sat in the dark and dreamed. But one day he woke up and began to apply himself. He wanted to make his mother proud. Like

Sidney, he loved his mother though he pretended to hate her, and luckily when he looked for a wife he found somebody just like his mother, only blonder and prettier. (That is probably why Mickey's kids are prettier than he is.) He thought he could have his cake and eat it too—but no, I am confusing Mickey with Sidney; Sidney is the one that likes cookies, and cake too—Mickey thought he could *reasonably accommodate* all his dreams at the same time. He could have a woman who was like his mother and yet not like his mother; he could make money and have fun too. He would become an entertainment lawyer! A dream of a job, and dreams on the job too. At least that was what Mickey thought. He didn't know he couldn't just turn down the lights in his office and pretend he was someplace else. He didn't realize that banks would want to finance so many horror movies. His dreams died, and so did Mickey; but nobody noticed, not even Mickey.

The foregoing is the kind of poetic nonsense Guy might write, when he is not trying to make a quick buck writing mystery novels. Police procedurals are not Guy's forte; his last mystery had a faulty plot; Guy is really a poet. It would be just like him to endow Mickey's life with a pathos that does not exist; he would like to think of Mickey as a failed poet, or a failed genius, or at the very least as a failed movie-mogul. Or even, if he stretched his imagination to include the non-pretty in this category, as a failed movie star. But Guy is more interested in the nymphomaniacal Ken Grabber than he is in Mickey Plotnick; his imaginings would not do Mickey justice. Mickey is not a failure at anything; he is too ruthless. And while Mickey is not exactly a movie star, he does have an important role in a movie, and this is part of his secret.

Of course there have been very few clues, up to this point, that would logically lead you to this conclusion. But can you expect clues when a plot does not exist? You can only expect facts. You know that Mickey helps to finance movie deals, horror flicks, and that production on one of these flicks was held up due to a shortage of bats. That might be funny, but it is also serious. Time is money. Money is important. In the end, the flick was finished.

Aha! you might think. Somewhere they came up with more bats. In your imagination you see Mrs. Plotnick. She is the dark horse. Nobody has seen the old bat. She is blind to Mickey's doings, blind as a bat. Mrs. Plotnick is a bat; Mickey's secret is that he is married to a bat.

But your imagination is wrong. Mrs. Plotnick is not a dark horse; she is a red herring. Mickey is the bat. Not only is he a bat; he is a vampire, that species of bat that feeds on the blood of others. Yes, yes, of course, you may be saying; all lawyers are vampires. But not all lawyers snub you in the hall; not all lawyers get parts as extras in Chase Manhattan's latest horror flick. You persist in disbelief: why insist that Mickey Plotnick is a bat, when there is a horror lurking in everything? There is horror in Ken Grabber's nymphomania; there is something horrifying about Sidney's cold-blooded search for a blonde Protestant; there is something horrible about proofreading, and messengering, and advertising, and law, and any number of gainful occupations. And then you might think about Ed and Vladimir, and try to shift the blame onto these two innocents, simply because you recall that they are Slavic, and that in Romania, a semi-Slavic country, there exists a province called Transylvania.

But all this is abstract, poetic thinking. Mickey Plotnick really is a bat; take my word for it, or take a look at him. Those gimlet eyes only really see in the dark. But he's never asleep on the job. When production was held up on the horror flick because the producers were short of bats, Mickey secretly volunteered his services; he arranged that filming of the scene would take place at night, and he duly showed up on the set. He had his moment of glory, or

155

fifteen minutes of fame, if you want to be exact about it—
the bats were a fairly important part of the picture.
Mickey was too modest to dream of stardom (Guy would
say); he never thought he might someday be a character
in a story; so he just played himself, in the movies, and
got paid handsomely for it.

Mickey's out for blood, but what of it? Sidney likes
cookies, and Ken Grabber drinks too much, and for all we
know Mr. Ed is a horse addict. All of these are lonely
occupations. But Mickey—dead if not buried, bereft of the
imaginary Mrs. Plotnick and the sham children—Mickey
is always in search of his perfect partner. His energy, his
power depend on it; so does any remaining resemblance to
the boy he once was. . . . For all we know Mickey might
like the blood of a poet, or a nymphomaniac, or an innocent. Guy and Ken Grabber think they have escaped in
time, but bats can easily fly from building to building. . . . Mickey's secret life is a nocturnal one; you
never know whom he might visit, while they are sleeping,
innocently. It is a nocturnal life, and therefore illogical;
you never know when Mickey might wake up and see
something, or someone, he's never really seen before; you
never know when he might realize how much he desires
the life of that stranger; you never know what secrets, or
tears, might be spilled upon the pillow, along with a certain necessary amount of blood.

Visitation of the Ghost

ONE DARK stormy night, a ghost appeared to two girls, separately, as befitting their very separate identities; they, and their ghosts, had little in common. But before they retired to their beds to face that ghost (or ghosts), they talked together. Their conversation turned often to reminiscence, as is often the case with people who are trying to get to know one another—everything tumbling out in an endless confession which (one hopes) will elicit mutual sympathy, confirm shared experience, or reduce the burden of guilt under which so many of us live. And if the conversation was also, untypically, tinged with the macabre—perhaps that was because of the storm.

One, Shelley, was studying Eastern mysticism these days, she said—all those Indian cats. She could rattle off their difficult Indian names with semi-reverent intonation. Not to slight the rest of the Occult. For instance, she knew a dark man in her dreams; she knew who he was and what he was up to. She recognized him no matter what his disguise, because he always had dark hair, and he was always jeering at her, telling her to give up. But she resisted him. She wanted to go to law school—and not just any law school, it had to be a top one. And she would!

Marjorie, who was not nearly so psychic, had no such

dream-man to tell Shelley about. All she could think of, in her own experience, was a cardboard art-print (anonymous artist) she had hanging on the wall between her mirror and closet. It depicted a young woman sitting upright in her fluffy four-poster bed, staring with surprise or terror (it was hard to tell) at a little red troll perched on a chair at the foot of the bed. A friend of hers from college had given it to her, saying it reminded her of Marjorie. Those were Marjorie's nervous-virgin days, also her take-offense days, and she was sure she didn't like the implication. Was sexual temptation, figuratively speaking, a little red troll? She thought that notion too fanciful.

—She thought he'd look more like an ominous dark-haired man, like Shelley's ominous dark-haired man, except Shelley had said specifically that he was trying to prevent her from going to law school, which didn't seem to have much to do with sex. No, and anyway, this girl was not repressed enough to dream up agents of sexual temptation, if Marjorie could believe everything she'd been saying. This girl Shelley, who said she'd thought about changing her name to Isis (a princess of the tarot deck) but then changed her mind (she was feeling bitter about the tarot lately, because it lied; she was better off trusting her own intuitive feelings) and so was still, plainly, Shelley— this girl was more than a little intimidating. All that talk about popularity, how disagreeable. Until fairly recently, Marjorie had no store of similar stories of amorous conquest, decline and fall (oh, these popular girls always thought themselves so unfortunate to have suffered the break-up, the brush-off, the bring-down), but she had heard it all before. She was a good listener, occasionally also a cynical one.

"A little dark man, huh?" said Marjorie with a derisive smile. "And who might he be?"

"Just part of myself," Shelley said. "Did you think I meant it literally?" She snorted.

"I don't know," Marjorie said. Because there is no way of knowing what people mean, when you don't know them well.

"It's like your will-to-fail," Shelley explained. "Once, when I was starting to do yoga, he tried to run me over with a station wagon. He said: So you want peace, huh? I'll give you peace!"

"Why does he always have dark hair?" Marjorie asked. "Because you do?"

"Who knows," said Shelley shortly.

As it turned out, that was a pertinent question to ask Shelley, if also a touchy one. Shelley had these thoughts on the subject of hair, which she delivered in a logical order: 1. Her hair was horribly short, so short she looked like a goon; 2. Men usually like long hair on women, so they can play around with it; 3. When you have short hair you need to wear more makeup, because more of your face shows; 4. She, Shelley, wore a lot of makeup for that reason, and also because she liked playing around with it, but mainly because no matter what she would always feel she was ugly as a witch; 5. She would always think she was so ugly because her stepmother used to tell her so. In fact, her stepmother actually had made her ugly one time by chopping off all of Shelley's hair.

It all came down to the stepmother.

"I was about thirteen then," Shelley continued, "which is just the age when you want to look nice, have boys notice you. And my stepmother made me get my hair cut real short. She cut all of my hair off.

"I cried and cried, I begged my father not to let her do it, but he let her anyway. I'll never forgive either of them. You know, my stepmother came to me a few years later and said: Will you forgive me for what I did to you? For cutting off your hair? And I said: No, never."

Marjorie pressed for details. How? Why?

161

"Jealousy," Shelley informed her. "She wanted her own daughter to look prettier, that was it. She was prettier anyway. I was kind of gawky, an ugly duckling in those days, but I was beginning to shape up. My stepmother didn't want me to look pretty—anyway I was my father's favorite.

"Hey!" Shelley said, sitting upright, as if she'd seen a ghost. "You don't know how mean she could be. She'd kick my brother and me out of the house and tell us not to come back. She told us we were ugly and worthless and stupid.

"She made my father take me to a barber, and they cut it short, but still with style: a pixie cut. But when we got home my stepmother took one look at me and said it wasn't short enough. She took me out to the backyard and she whacked it off, in front of all my friends yet. And my father just stood by and watched, he didn't stop her, because he didn't want another divorce."

Marjorie hadn't thought stepmothers were so wicked, in real life.

"I had a very unhappy childhood," said Shelley.

"So did I," Marjorie said.

But she felt at a loss. She had no stepmother stories, no archetypal traumas of castration and/or rejection. Again, Shelley had outdone her! That is, if you could believe Shelley. Something was missing: the horror was missing. Shelley's tales, as told by Shelley anyway, sounded dull, flat, almost clinical. Marjorie had heard terrible things, things that should inspire horror, pity, disbelief—and yet, truly, she felt none of it but the disbelief. Here was Shelley, rattling off her past as if by rote, the pertinent elements being plot, setting, caricature—and these were supposed to elicit the proper response. Now with Marjorie it was the other way around; what she remembered of her own childhood was the horror itself—and it was all the more genuine for its vagueness. Sometimes little anec-

Visitation of the Ghost

dotes surfaced from the void—and they were only about unimportant people and events. But she couldn't tell why she'd been such a miserable child, except in the haziest feelings, the ghostliest contours. . . .

"Nobody liked me," she said finally. "They didn't like me at school. They called me a brain and made jokes about me.

"I was always the last one picked for softball teams," Marjorie concluded.

"Always?" queried Shelley.

"Well, sometimes second to last," Marjorie admitted. "Sometimes I'd be lucky, there'd be someone weirder or worse in gym—there was nothing worse than being weird or bad in gym. Or smelling bad and wearing funny clothes. Once I was saved by a Yugoslavian girl who'd just moved into the neighborhood. They liked her even less than me, because she wore these funny braids."

"I was funny," Shelley said. "But they loved me. I was a real cut-up. We were always getting into trouble, my brother and me. We were holy terrors. The teachers didn't know what to do with me."

Marjorie thought about Larry Hooper, who'd been one of the smartest guys in school—a brain on a level with her own. But he got away with it because he was funny. And she'd always been too shy, a late-bloomer. . . . What had become of Larry Hooper?

"I was a terror at home," Marjorie said. "That's where I took out my temper. At school I was too smart and sweet and good, so of course my teachers loved me and everyone else couldn't stand me. When I went home, though, I raised Cain. I'd put my brother and sister up to all kinds of mischief—"

"Like what?" Shelley wanted to know.

Marjorie thought a moment. "I don't know, maybe I just fought with them. But we must have made some trouble together, because everyone in the family called me

163

The Ringleader. And I used to pull tantrums all the time. . . .

"But I don't blame my parents," Marjorie concluded. "They'd go to Open House and listen to my teachers rave about me, and they'd think: Are they talking about our Marjorie? The same child? But they never gave me away. At least I don't think so. They just waited until they came home and told me and we had a good laugh about it."

"There's no mercy in the universe," Shelley said, misquoting one of her masters. "My stepmother had no mercy at all. Listen to what she did. One day, I was about twelve, a strange lady came to visit us, and my father introduced her as a friend of the family. She started petting my brother and me, her hands were all over us. And do you know, we were so starved for affection, we let her. We had no idea who she was, why she was doing this. When she left my stepmother said—she was so jealous: Ha-ha, do you know who that lady was? That was your mother!

"She told us just like that. That was so mean of her."

"You didn't know your own mother?"

"Hell no," said Shelley, "I'd seen her in my dreams, but only in my dreams. I was just two years old when she left. One day she left us alone in the house and didn't come back. We were only babies, and she was an alcoholic. Just like my stepmother. My dad always marries alcoholics."

Shelley went on about her mother. She'd seen her a couple of times since that first reunion. Her mother was still good-looking, still alcoholic, still unstable. Also (lucky for Shelley) sometimes guilty. Once, when Shelley and her brother shared an apartment, the mother sent them a truckload of imported furniture, paid for by one of the boyfriends she lived with on a rotating basis.

"And then you should have seen what my father sent us," Shelley continued. "They both have a load of guilt to pay off. I'm not going to make it any easier for them, either. Sometimes I feel guilty myself, for calling my father whenever I want money, but after all he owes it to us. He'll never be able to deny me. He always sends more than I ask for.

"I know I blow a lot of money," Shelley admitted, "but it runs in the family. You should see how my father throws it away. I can't help it. Anyway, I'm twenty-two, I don't want to look like a goon. I want to have decent clothes.

"My stepmother used to make me wear things from the Salvation Army. She'd buy nice things for her own daughter, but we ran around in rags.

"But you should see me now, parading around in my furs! I have to admit it, I get a kick out of making people jealous."

"Yeah," said Marjorie, "I'm still jealous of girls with nice clothes, because I still don't have them. I'm just a poor student . . . not that we were so poor when I was little, it was just that my mother was a cheapskate! Or she didn't know. . . . I never dressed the right way. In sixth grade all the girls wore mohair cardigans and white blouses with the shirttails out, penny loafers, madras purses. I had to fight for penny loafers, because my mother didn't think they provided enough arch-support. I never did get a mohair sweater."

All of a sudden, talking about mohair sweaters, Marjorie thought about Marcia Cameron. Now, Marcia had worn mohair, but she hadn't been popular, at least not until seventh grade, when for some unknown reason Scott Lewis (whose reputation as a great playboy dated back to fifth grade at least) fell for her. Lewis was a legend; if "Louie Louie" hadn't been written about him, everyone knew it was his theme song. And in seventh grade, the Great Lewis was actually sending love letters to Marcia Cameron, and Marcia was suddenly popular. Never mind that she had bad skin. Never mind that Lewis must have suddenly realized that she had bad skin, whereupon he broke up with her. Marcia went on to new boyfriends. Marcia had finally made it.

Marjorie tried to remember why Marcia had been a semi-outcast in the first place. It wasn't because she was smart. Marjorie had thought she'd smelled funny, but maybe that was only the musty odor of the laminated paperback they'd shared in an English class. It was probably because Marcia was a hillbilly, from Kentucky or Tennessee, and because she tried to scare people silly with her superstitious stories.

"I knew a girl who believed that if a ghost visited your bed in the middle of the night, someone in your family would die the next day unless you repeated a secret Latin prayer proclaiming the power of God," Marjorie told Shelley.

"You're not going to tell ghost stories," Shelley protested. "Not during a storm. I'm feeling kind of creepy already."

"It's not really a ghost story," Marjorie said. "Nothing else happens, at least I can't remember it. This girl Marcia swore she'd seen this ghost. Lucky for her, she remembered the prayer and prevented any deaths. But she warned us, if we woke up in the night to see a shadowy figure standing before us, that's who he was, and it was our duty to repeat the prayer, no matter how terrified we were."

"What was the prayer?" asked Shelley, for future reference.

Marjorie shrugged. "I don't remember. I don't think I even knew it by heart then. Some Latin mumbo jumbo. Everyone thought she was crazy."

"I don't know if I believe in ghosts or not," Shelley said. "At least not Christian ones. I'm surrounded by spirits all the time, I'm a Pisces, but they're all just like

166

the dark-haired guy in my dreams. They're either from my past lives or my subconscious. If I saw a ghost before me in the middle of the night I'd think it was a man.''

"A man?'' asked Marjorie.

"Yeah. You know what my boyfriend did, before I even knew him? We were living in the same house, but we didn't really know each other yet. One night I woke up and there he was with his hand underneath my nightgown. I said: What the fuck do you think you're doing? Get out of here! And he said: I can't help myself, you're so beautiful, I want to make love to you.''

Marjorie shuddered.

Shelley went on: "He kept playing around with me, and I kept telling him to get out of there, and finally he did. It's amazing we ever started going out together. I hated him, I thought he was the biggest jerk—but I don't know, we started kidding around, and a couple of days later we finally did get together.''

Marjorie had never been taken by surprise by man or ghost, though once she had been waiting for one. When she was twelve or thirteen she had been convinced that there was a man living in the basement, a man who prowled the house every night. Every night she would wake up and listen for the slightest noise that would betray his presence. She heard footsteps—or doors creaking—or locks picked, even; there was always the chance he didn't live in the basement, but entered illicitly each night. Her body clenched and sweating, she would lie perfectly still for hours, lying in wait for him. She stilled her heartbeat the better to hear his.

It ended soon after her father took her down to the basement and showed her it was only the furnace acting up.

But every fantasy has its basis in fact, and the fact was what Marjorie decided to tell Shelley:

"You have to be careful about who's living in your house,'' Marjorie said. "A long time ago, about ten years

167

ago I think, there was this story in the newspaper about a man who woke up in the middle of the night when someone tapped him on the shoulder. And he turned around, expecting to see his wife, but instead this hag was standing over him. It turned out she'd been living in his basement for months.''

''Sometimes you have no control over who's living in your house,'' Shelley said. ''My father used to come into my room, too. When I was pretty young. I'd wake up and there he'd be sitting on the edge of my bed with his hands on me.''

Marjorie knew she couldn't ask just what it was Shelley's father was doing. So she said, ''What did you do?''

''I'd tell him to get out. I said: What the fuck do you think you're doing? Leave me alone!'' Shelley stopped. ''That's why my father can't refuse me anything. He knows he owes it to me.

''I hated my father for so long, you can't know,'' she said. ''But I got over it.''

''Yes,'' Marjorie said briskly, ''you have to get over things, that's the new theory. Theories change, people change—we're not the same people we were a long time ago. We're grown up, we can't go around blaming everything on our childhood. I try not to harp on it.''

''Well,'' Shelley said dubiously, ''sometimes it really does have a bad effect on you, all your life.''

And then, not trusting each other any more, they went to their beds.

Shelley, being psychic, met her ghost in her dreams. It was none other than her familiar dark-haired man. She faced him bravely. But this time he did not torment her. He appeared at her door, calm and gentle, with a book in his hands. And when he spoke, his voice no longer hissed with seduction, but instead reassured, comforted.

''He's finally on my side,'' Shelley told Marjorie the

168

next day. "That book he was carrying, maybe it was a Bible, maybe some other kind of wise book. Anyway, I know it's because I decided to be a religion major. After talking last night I started thinking about it, I thought I'd switch from philosophy to religion. It must be the right decision, because that guy wasn't scary anymore. Everything's going to be all right."

Marjorie could not bring herself to repeat her own vision. She felt too uneasy; things had not resolved themselves yet. Last night, she had awakened into a nightmare. Something, some unilluminated being, was hovering at the foot of her bed. At once Marjorie remembered the story Marcia Cameron had told, but she could not remember the prayer. And if she didn't, someone in her family would die the very next day. She mulled this over calmly, as she stared into the darkness to keep her ghost at bay. And then—with a thrill of terror, a giggle of elation—she turned on her light.

It was only then that the horror began. What have I done, Marjorie asked herself with dread, with guilt. She had remembered that she needed to say the prayer, that failing to do so meant someone in her family would die— but somehow she hadn't recognized the danger. Or worse, she hadn't cared—she *wanted* one of them to die— Who would it be? Did her ghost give her a clue? Yes, she had known who, then; she had known at the instant it appeared; but now, with the ghost vanished, the lights on, everything was obscure.

All day long Marjorie walked in dread, the dread of a telegram or telephone message confirming a death in the family. But none came.

None came, all were well, the danger was over, yet still Marjorie was troubled. Why had she risked it, why had she giggled at the thought of killing off someone she loved? Unless she hadn't believed it was a ghost—

But she had.

169

Marjorie searched the literature of psychic phenomena for an explanation. Nowhere could she find a legend like the one Marcia Cameron had told her about so long ago. Perhaps it was too old-fashioned; the occult these days was psychologically up-to-date. Perhaps it was as Shelley said; the dark powers were your own. Take, for instance, the approach of the instruction manual Marjorie bought, *Your Psychic Powers (And How To Develop Them)*. Now it concedes that ghosts, or apparitions, are generally phantasms of the dead. But it also classifies as ghosts those cases of "experimental apparitions" in which the spirit of a sleeper who has been mesmerized or otherwise put in a trance state is projected to a certain locality, where it is seen by those present.

In fact (p. 241): "apparitions may be induced experimentally by willing very strongly, just as you are falling asleep, that you will appear to a certain person at a certain time, and if this is properly managed, it will be successful in a number of cases."

Marjorie was confused. She couldn't imagine why another living soul would want to project himself, without his body, into her bedroom. And since she kept her door locked, no intruder could have entered, no sleepwalker would have wandered in. There had been no body but Marjorie's in the room, and while she had sleepwalked in her childhood, she had given it up years ago. . . .

Suddenly the logical answer appeared. Marjorie reasoned: If someone willed that ghost to appear—and she saw the ghost—then maybe that ghost was none other than an incarnation of Marjorie Appearing to Herself. And if Marjorie summoned her ghost only to make it vanish, maybe she was banishing it forever. She thought this explained why she hadn't repeated the prayer. After all, she could have remembered it, if she'd wanted to dig deeply into her past. But that was just what she didn't want to do. Yes, Marjorie knew now who that ghost was;

she knew the child who'd been lingering too long, whose time had come, who was destined to die. . . .

(But Shelley kept seeing that dark-haired man in her dreams. He'd gone back to jeering at her. "Oh," she told Marjorie, "he approved of the religion, but that doesn't keep him from giving me trouble about everything else."

And then she would go on about her stepmother.)

Budapest Dangereux

ELSE BERGER was, by all accounts, a particularly good psychic, and reliable. Though she did not mind being called a fortune-teller, she did not operate out of any tawdry tent, but rather a clean and unadorned office in her townhouse on the east side of the city. She had been recommended by several of Henny's friends, so Henny called for a consultation.

Lately Henny had been having troubling dreams—not dreams exactly. But in the half-awake state immediately preceding sleep she would be suddenly visited by strange faces floating up at her in the dark. Right away Henny would open her eyes wide and they would disappear, but she could not instantly shake off the feeling that these faces were familiar—as familiar as they were terrifying. And yet on the evidence of a quick glimpse, none of the faces resembled anybody Henny was currently acquainted with.

On the other hand, it was true that Henny had a terrible memory for faces. It was possible she was half-remembering a few insignificant figures from the many shadowy years that made up her past. But Henny did not think so. For the most part her life had been a pleasant one; meeting up with old friends, even in her sleep, would probably be pleasant too. There would be no reason to run

173

away from them before they could be recognized! In the face of this inescapable logic, it occurred to Henny that there was bound to be a much more disturbing explanation for her apparitions. That was why she thought she should consult Else.

Else Berger was a Hungarian, originally from Budapest. In her spare time—which was not bountiful, since she made quite a decent living from seeing the future—she was writing a book entitled *Budapest Dangereux*. Else would not describe this book, or divulge anything about its contents, except to say that it was "historical." Nobody had dared open the book—seemingly an ordinary blank book with fleur-de-lis covers—but there were those of her clients who suspected that it was really a secret handbook of the occult and not a historical romance at all. All of these doubting clients were sure that Else was not, at heart, a romantic type; and for further proof there was the title. What could have been dangerous about Budapest, and to whom? The danger of Budapest had to be a secret, other-worldly one, apparent only to people like Else. Whereas to the ordinary observer (Else's clients agreed) Budapest was a charming city, at least it had been charming in the days before it was hidden behind the Iron Curtain. And Else Berger had left long ago, so her memories, if not her family, were probably intact.

In fact Else Berger's family had all been "killed in the war." That was as much as she would say. Else did not dwell on her own past, nor on anybody else's either: she was clearly impatient, for example, with modern theories on the haunting power of an unhappy childhood. She was, on the other hand, more than a little interested in (and knowledgeable about) past lives, lives lived before the present one. This made her the ideal person to consult, thought Henny's friends. Because Henny had no doubt been remembering, in the period just before sleep, some of the people she had known in a previous life.

In this life Henny was the proprietor of a tea shop. Being a woman of Hungarian descent and expansive, Bohemian temperament, she naturally attracted eccentric patrons to her tea shop and befriended them. Although American-born, Henny was perhaps more suited than Else to the life of a fortune-teller. Most of her patrons were devotees of the art of fortune-telling, so she might have had a ready-made clientele; and then it so happened that Henny looked a bit like a gypsy. She was stout, with a huge bouffant of hennaed hair and multiple chains of cheap jewels roped around her neck. But that was as far as she went, because lacking any psychic talent that was as far as she could go. Years ago, for the sake of her friends, she had installed in the tea shop a woman who read cards. This service had proved successful, but then the woman died in an unforeseen car accident. Henny had felt it unlucky to replace her.

After that her patrons had their fortunes told elsewhere, mostly at Else Berger's office.

When Henny arrived at Else Berger's office for her appointment, Else was taken aback. She had heard of Henny, proprietress of a tea shop known for its European civility, its pastries of Hungarian origin and its patrons of intellect. All this Else knew, and sometimes she had been tempted to visit Henny's shop—although ever since arriving in America she had cut herself off from anything remotely Hungarian. Even her accent barely betrayed her. While Else would have appreciated the tea shop's atmosphere of good fellowship and lively manners, she had no desire to eat Hungarian pastries. Why then did Henny look so familiar?

Henny could see that Else thought she recognized her, but because she had such a terrible memory her own lack of recognition did not trouble her. Else was small and slight and pale—ordinary, impossible to pick out in a

175

crowd. Politeness, however, prompted Henny to inquire, "Have we met before?"

"We must have," said Else.

The logical place for them to have met was the tea shop. Henny was about to suggest it, when Else seemed to jump ahead and unexpectedly asked how long Henny had owned the tea shop. "Ten years," answered Henny automatically; it was easy to remember because she could date her new career back to just after her husband's death.

Else felt at a loss. That was not long enough ago. She had had the unmistakable impression that her memory of Henny dated back long ago, perhaps back to those foggy days when she was a young war refugee. Else so imperfectly remembered her state of mind in those days that it was possible that she had once deliberately set out to visit a Hungarian tea shop, hoping to be reminded of an earlier, happier time in her homeland. . . . But apparently Henny's tea shop had not existed then, at least not as Henny's.

"You do look familiar," Else said, "perhaps I have seen you at a concert or a film." But Henny did not think so. "I rarely go out," she explained kindly, "don't you think perhaps it was at my tea shop after all?"

"Of course," Else said reassuringly, got hold of herself, and turned the tables: she asked Henny if she would like some tea.

Henny said she would. The tea, an English blend, calmed them both. Else imagined drinking tea at Henny's place; it no longer seemed so impossible. In fact it was probably not so long ago at all. Else would not admit it to Henny, it might undermine her confidence, but there were days that Else seemed to blindly wander the city, in neighborhoods strange to her; but afterwards, even the next day, she could barely remember where she had been.

All her life Henny had suffered from a terrible, aching

176

wanderlust, but she had never traveled much. Those places she had visited, however, mostly cities on the Eastern seaboard and a resort in Mexico, were vivid in her memory. It was only people she had trouble remembering, she had only the haziest recollection of the people she'd met in her travels. Henny was sorry about this haziness only in the case of a Mexican man she had met forty years ago during the war. Sometimes she would wear a red appliquéd Mexican jacket (a souvenir) to bed with her, and think about the man—a waiter at the resort restaurant—Miguel? She could not be sure that that was his name. Nor could she exactly picture what he looked like, except that he had a mustache, and was dark and broodingly handsome like a gypsy—like a Mexican, actually.

Some of the faces that tried to haunt Henny in the dark were brooding, but she knew none of them were Miguel's.

During the war Mexico was the perfect place for a vacation, mainly because there was nowhere else to go. Henny liked Mexico, even though she knew she would never belong there; it was safe. After the war ended, she could have traveled elsewhere, to Europe, but visiting the land of her grandparents held little charm for her, since her grandparents, presumably, were dead. Mexico, of course, was still there, and she did always mean to go back and relive those happy times, but something held her back; perhaps her husband.

Else Berger had never had a husband. As a refugee after the war she had met a psychoanalyst, a naturalized American who had left his homeland before the war, on a premonition. But apart from that premonition, Else decided, he lacked imagination, and besides that he wanted children. Else told him she could not bear the thought of having children.

Now that she was sixty, well past the danger of future Bergers, Else felt free to indulge her appreciation of other people's children. She was particularly fond of the English grandchildren of one of her clients, Maria Edge. Maria's daughter Carol, born in Connecticut, had come to Else years ago on a whim; she was unhappy in love. Soon after, on Else's advice, Carol had married an Englishman and moved to England to raise her future family there. Ever since, Carol and her husband and her three children had lived happily in the English countryside, in the land of their ancestors, and every summer Else went to visit them.

This fortunate family was, Else felt, one of her greater successes. But Carol's mother, Maria Edge, was not. Perhaps it was because Maria was just her age that Else felt impatient with Maria's worry about the future. After all, Maria was remarkably well-preserved and in excellent health. Nothing had ever gone wrong in her life, but despite this Maria had always worried about the future; and in recent years this worry had metamorphosed into a reckless, insatiable desire to know the worst.

At times Else was tempted to make up horrible fortunes for Maria, to truly scare her; but Else was too reliable to lie. Besides, Maria's vision of the worst was not all that bad, so Else could, in all conscience, tell her quite enough to satisfy her fears.

Despite her morbid streak, Maria Edge never asked about her past lives. Else knew why she did not feel she had to. In the hallway of her great old Connecticut house hung a row of portraits that documented the history of her family. The family was not only illustrious but also so real and personal, to Maria, that she could not help but feel that she had, in some guise or other, lived in every generation—even her mother's and father's. She had once confided this extraordinary idea to Else, and Else had told her it was impossible. She knew all about Maria Edge's family, and none of her aunts, or even uncles, had died just before Maria's birth. But what about when I was a baby and couldn't remember anything, Maria said, and yet I remember living the life of my Aunt Frances, driving in a roadster with a silk scarf tied around my head. Impossible, Else said gently, you cannot be two people at once.

Finally, Maria Edge, not being a stupid woman, was convinced by the strength of this argument, and concluded that it was only the sense of the past she felt. And Else assured her she knew the feeling; whenever she was in England she had the uncanny, lovely assurance that she had, in a previous life, belonged there.

But while she was drinking tea with Henny, even English tea, Else did not feel very English. She was studying the downward curve of Henny's flashing eyes—a curve not at all English, but resembling her own—when the telephone rang. It was Maria Edge, an unexpected pleasure: Carol and her family were visiting from England, and Else was invited to come to Connecticut for the weekend. Else gladly accepted.

When she got off the phone she felt lighthearted, as if granted a last-minute reprieve. I must be working too hard, Else thought. With reluctance she shook off her reveries of Connecticut and turned back to Henny. According to her method, Else concentrated on Henny's face and hands. But the feeling she had had of having seen Henny before had faded. And while she did see a downward curve of the outer eye that resembled her own, Else was no longer interested in discovering any family connection. That had nothing to do with Henny's problem. Henny was a sixty-year-old American of Hungarian extraction, Hungarian-Jewish extraction; but what could that extraction have to do with Henny's haunting faces?

Haunting faces, Else told herself, had to do with a past life. The trouble was she had no idea what Henny's past life might be.

Else was on the verge of panic, on the edge of utter

179

blankness. But she was a good businesswoman; she knew what to do. She drew her face into an expression of authority, and then cast her eyes downward. She picked up Henny's hands, marked with several diamond rings and liver spots, and said, "It is not surprising that you are troubled by your sleep. All your life you have been surrounded by the disturbances of sleep."

This was a shot in the dark. But after all, sleep disturbances included everything from nightmares to insomnia to sleepwalking, and nobody was exempt from an occasional nightmare. At times Else suspected that her own daytime wanderings were some frightening kind of non-nocturnal somnambulism. Else was thinking of herself again, lost in the mists of some imperfect memory, and then suddenly she came to and looked at Henny's face. It was a look Else knew well, had seen on the face of every client who returned to her: she had hit upon some awful truth, and they could not help themselves from wanting to find out more. . . .

Henny could not help thinking about Arthur. She knew he had nothing to do with what was happening to her now, if anything it was Miguel who occupied her thoughts, but nevertheless Else had proved she knew something about her—and that something was Arthur. Henny's husband Arthur had died, ten years ago, at a relatively young age. His death was unexpected—a car accident. He had been in the garage trying to start the car in the cold, and had suddenly fallen asleep. The gas—carbon monoxide—had poisoned him. While his death was unexpected, the possibility of his dying in such an accident was not, because he happened to suffer from narcolepsy.

It was for this reason that Henny and Arthur never traveled abroad. Henny promised she would watch over him every step of the way, and protect him, but that did not convince Arthur. He remained deathly afraid of his powerlessness at the hands of foreigners, though at home he was adventurous enough to drive his car in the winter. I can take care of myself, Arthur would insist, as long as I'm in familiar territory.

"You see, I know everything," Else said soothingly.

But this remark did not have the desired hypnotic effect. Instead Henny burst out crying.

When she stopped crying for a moment she said, "It wasn't my fault, and anyway he died ten years ago. Usually I can forget it. But when I can't help thinking about it, I also can't help feeling miserable."

After another cup of tea Henny calmed down and told Else enough to demystify her. "Of course I couldn't blame him for falling asleep," Henny said. "Nobody knew what caused it, so he couldn't help it. Still, he knew that someday he might fall asleep at just the wrong time, so how could he let it happen?"

Else reminded Henny that after all one day in winter, at home, in one's own garage, was very like another, and how could Arthur be expected to recognize the danger?

"That's true," Henny said. "We had so many years without any trouble to speak of. Why shouldn't he go start the car? I was off shopping, I didn't see the danger either. I didn't see the danger either," she repeated, for no reason, but dreamily, and suddenly Else saw a face of her own. The face was floating up in the light, a narrow strip of late sunlight and rare dust on Else's modern desk.

Being a shiny chrome, the desk made an admirable crystal ball. Up through the dust and light this face slowly became recognizable. Not surprisingly, Else saw, the face looked like Henny. But it was not Henny.

It was somebody else, somebody Else had known in her pre-refugee days. Else hated to think about that time and had nearly succeeded in forgetting it. As a consequence she had also nearly forgotten the old woman (a young Else had thought her old) who had once owned a tea shop in Budapest.

She might have been Henny's aunt, Else thought, an aunt she had never met, but one who had (for a time) lived the same kind of life—a pleasant life of tea and pastries. Was that why they looked so remarkably alike? Or was it only the downward curve of the outer corner of their eyes that set them apart and proclaimed them kin? But no, Else had that same curve, and yet she knew the tea shop lady had been no relation of anybody in the Berger family.

For a long moment Else sat transfixed by the face of Henny's possible aunt, but then she blinked, and in that instant the aunt disappeared.

Henny, not being psychic, did not see anything on Else's desk but a little dust, and she thought the ghostly look on Else's face was entirely normal for a fortune-teller. Obediently she waited for Else to go on, to tell her what to make of Arthur's death.

Finally Else stopped staring at her desk and turned to Henny and smiled, as if relieved to still find her there.

"Close the tea shop and go away," Else said in a low urgent whisper, "before it is too late."

Luckily she said it in Hungarian, so Henny had no idea what she was talking about. Otherwise she might have thought Else had gone mad. (The tea shop was, since Arthur's death, her whole life, and she saw no reason to leave it.) The fact that Else was suddenly speaking Hungarian was startling enough.

The look of utter incomprehension on Henny's face woke Else up. She realized that what had happened had happened, it was already too late; and why tell Henny about it? The fate she had thought she had foreseen, but

182

only remembered, was not Henny's. Henny was still alive.

"I was only talking to myself," Else said, "forgive me."

"I understand," Henny said kindly, "sometimes I do it myself. In English though. Arthur used to think it very strange of me."

"But entirely normal," Else rejoined. She got up and busied herself for several minutes making more tea. Already the idea of Budapest seemed very far away. She was worried about how to get rid of Henny, how to get herself out of the confusion she had created. Talking about sleep disturbances had been a mistake, she realized that now; and it had thrown Henny off the track too, with all this business about narcolepsy. . . . On the other hand, it was possible that Henny only saw faces in the dark because she was afraid to go to sleep and not wake up, like Arthur.

But then Henny said, as if reading her mind: "Sometimes I think it would be a blessing in disguise to be able to fall asleep instantly, like Arthur. I doubt whether Arthur ever saw any faces."

"No," Else agreed. "Narcolepsy may be a mystery but it is also a disease, nothing supernatural. Your visions, on the other hand, are easily explicable, and at the same time they have nothing to do with anything so ordinary as a bodily malady."

"They have to do with a past life, after all?" Henny asked eagerly.

"No doubt," Else said firmly. Now she was in more familiar territory.

"What past life?" Henny then asked.

Else was still not prepared to answer. Without thinking she looked down at her desk, and on its luminescent surface the face of Henny's aunt appeared again.

"A past life as a gypsy," Else said, averting her eyes

and looking into her teacup instead (although she had never studied the art of tea-leaf-reading).

This was of course a lie, but Else was powerless. She could not resist taking the safe and easy way out. Henny looked like a gypsy so in a past life she was a gypsy.

But this explanation seemed to please Henny. She thought this sounded plausible, and at the same time fascinating. Gypsies traveled a lot. They had also suffered, but only in recent memory, Henny thought, not long ago when she had lived as one.

Then she remembered her terror at seeing the dark brooding faces—the gypsy faces, she guessed. "Was it an unhappy life?" she wanted to know.

"Not at all," Else said smoothly. She continued automatically: "You are only afraid to see the faces because you are afraid to remember this life. And that is only because you have not yet accepted the idea that you have lived before. You are frightened by your imperfect memory and by a familiar unfamiliarity."

"I see," Henny said. "Tell me, then, what was my life as a gypsy like?"

But Else, seeing nothing, could invent no details. She vaguely remembered seeing gypsies in the streets of Budapest, years ago . . . but in those days, like now, she had led a civilized and insular life. She had never really known how the gypsies had lived, though of course she knew that some of the gypsy women made their fortunes by predicting false, pleasant futures. . . . It would have been simpler, Else told herself, if she had told Henny she had once been an Englishwoman. That was something Else knew about. But England was Else's; it meant too much to her, she took it too seriously to make believe that Henny had once lived there too.

Henny, for better or worse, had to be a gypsy.

"That life," she told Henny, "you can remember if you want to. Yes. You must remember it yourself." She felt a

184

small dark doubt, a sudden chill of premonition, as she said this; but perhaps that was only guilt, the unfamiliar sensation of having told a lie. . . . Luckily, before Henny could ask any more questions, her time was up.

But Henny was not unsatisfied. She did not wonder when she had lived, or where; gypsies were eternal, they lived everywhere. In her imagination, indifferent to history, the constraints of time and place did not exist. But she was eager for the pleasures of her past life to eventually reveal themselves, in the faces of all those she used to know and love. She was no longer afraid to see them. Else Berger, a reliable psychic, recommended by Henny's friends, had reassured her.

That night, and for several nights thereafter, Henny went to bed early in excited anticipation. She closed her eyes and tried to drift into the sea of pre-sleep.

Predictably, no gypsies immediately appeared to her. Instead, Henny found herself thinking about Miguel, or at least remembering the warmth of the Mexican sun, and a few moments later she would be lulled into a dreamless, full-bodied sleep.

Counting the days until her Connecticut weekend, Else Berger could not sleep. She sat up every night staring at the pages of the book she called *Budapest Dangereux*. But it was only a blank book with fleur-de-lis covers.

Once, long ago, she had meant to write it all down— the dawning sense of danger, of not being Hungarian enough; the deportations in the countryside; the gangs in the streets of Budapest, the machine-gun executions on the shores of the Blue Danube; and then traveling, traveling to foreign places, escaping—or not escaping. What a romance she would give them! Nobody in America had dreamed of what it had been like. And, after a time in America, neither did Else Berger, anymore. She buried

185

her memories and lived in the future—or, better, a past so distant, so abstract and impersonal that neither its horrors nor pleasures could be truly felt.

Yes; the pages of *Budapest Dangereux* were blank. Long ago Else had resigned herself to the idea of never writing the book; but she could not admit her fear to anybody else. In time, she thought, they would forget all about it. Some did. But every so often, one of her clients would ask her how her historical romance was coming along. They assured her they were eager to read all about dangerous Budapest; they made her promise to let them know the instant she had come to the end.

Henny was thinking about Miguel, one night, remembering the warmth of the Mexican sun forty years ago, but still not remembering Miguel's face. She wanted very much to remember Miguel's face.

In her sudden lust even the gypsies did not seem to matter much.

She decided that first she must set the scene; if she could see the place she might trick herself into seeing Miguel. And so she summoned up the resort where she had first glimpsed Miguel, in his waiter whites. But Miguel's white costume seemed to blur into the white facade of the resort, and then that too flashed by, and Henny felt she was hurtling down a long white tunnel—back into time? She was no longer in the Mexican resort, she didn't even feel like the same person. A younger person, maybe—at summer camp. When she was a teenager Henny had gone to summer camp.

It was then that Henny realized that in the logic of dreams, or even pre-dreams, what matters is not what you see but the words that describe them. It was not summer camp she was seeing, but another sort of camp. A gypsy camp, it must be.

At once Henny felt hot and cold, and her eyelids

186

twitched. She prepared herself to see a gypsy campfire and smiling faces dancing around. But when the faces appeared they were not smiling at all. As always, they were dark and brooding; they might have been Mexicans or gypsies, but they were not happy.

Else was wrong, Henny thought, the people I loved did suffer. . . . In quick succession each face swirled up to her in close-up, and none of them looked familiar until the last.

It's me, Henny thought, and she tried to force herself awake before she screamed.

She screamed anyway. The nightmare did not seem to have ended, Henny was not quite awake. She was certain she was dead: killed, gassed like Arthur and yet not like Arthur, but rather in a specific time and place, and for a specific reason—she had been a gypsy in the wrong kind of camp.

As if in a trance she dialed Else Berger's number.

Else Berger knew instantly who was calling her; she had been expecting the call. This was why, perhaps, she could not bring herself to go to Connecticut after all. . . .

For a moment or two, perhaps longer, Else listened as the voice screamed into her ear. She screamed back: you weren't a gypsy, admit it, you owned a tea shop in Budapest, I knew you. . . . But the voice did not seem to hear her. Like Henny, Else was not quite awake. When the present caught up with her, she realized that she hadn't screamed back after all; but there was no need to. She knew she could comfort Henny; now it was all a matter of logistics.

"You are alive," she told Henny, "you cannot have been killed in a concentration camp."

Curiously, the case of Maria Edge—such an utterly different case—floated into Else's mind. Like Maria Edge, Henny would not believe Else until she was reminded that

187

she could not be two people in two places at the same time. It was an inescapable fact.

"But I must have died at some time," Henny said finally.

It was as if this had just occurred to her. But even Maria Edge, Else thought, expected to die. "Of course," she told Henny, "but it was not in a concentration camp during the war. You died . . . at the turn of the century. A good forty years before the war. By the time of the war, you were living a new life, in America. You were lucky, you were safe."

"Of course," Henny repeated. But in the aftermath of her nightmare her early, pleasant life did not seem quite real. It was all a haze to her, all those years before the war was over and she grew up and married Arthur. Where had she been, what had she been doing?

Then she remembered Mexico. "I was in Mexico during the war," she told Else. "We had to go there, there was nowhere else to go, but it was very nice. I remember it quite well." She could feel Miguel's body, a faceless warmth touching her. It was proof.

The Mystery of Madame Kitten

Nowadays, Madame Kitten is not here. It is a great mystery what has happened to her.

PART 1. PARIS

It began happening in Paris, all of Madame Kitten's past. Everything that ever happened to her had happened in Paris. Yes; once upon a time Madame Kitten lived in Paris. At the time Madame Kitten did not think of Paris this way. She considered herself a citizen of larger worlds. Paris was just a place where she had worked too hard, made too many mistakes, known too many people. At work, lying flat on her back looking up at the ceiling, she used to wish she were looking at the stars. So after work did she go outside and look at them? No. She'd lost the urge. Or it was daylight. It was the wrong time and it was the wrong place too. It was Paris. In Paris even the stars weren't far away enough.

Now it is true that most Parisians want to get away from Paris, especially in the summer. Those who can't get away get postcards from those who do. Most Parisians received colorful postcards from friends vacationing on the Riviera; Madame Kitten preferred to receive mysterious signals from Space.

Mysterious signals from Space are usually dark and amorphous and as such cannot compete with picture post-cards in an ordinary story.

Madame Kitten was not ordinary but she was still a Parisian. Not only did she have friends who vacationed on the Riviera; she had also met many men who had passed through Paris, though she couldn't remember most of them.

Madame Kitten tried very hard not to remember most of them.

Still, when you meet so many people who are coming and going and so many people meet you, there is a chance in heaven that one day you will get a mysterious signal in the form of a postcard from one of them.

In Madame Kitten's mail, forwarded many times, was a glossy black-and-white postcard with the actual title "Those Mysterious Signals from Space."

This Space was filled with Stars: a mass of tiny famous faces surrounding a hermaphrodite Botticelli Venus.

Beside the Stars were some real stars, also a cross, an eye, a number or two, a number of other signs and symbols. None of these signaled anything mysterious to Madame Kitten. She had decided long ago that there were too many symbols in the world. En masse, they lacked mystery and therefore power. Madame Kitten had lived the life of a symbol for many years, and yet she still hadn't had the power to go off to the Riviera without her pimp.

Now it is no mystery that Madame Kitten was an ex-prostitute.

There are twenty thousand prostitutes in Paris, almost as many prostitutes in Paris as symbols in the world, but in this case there really is no power in numbers.

As an *ex*-prostitute, Madame Kitten had newfound power—earning power—should she ever care to write her memoirs. Of course she would have to write them anonymously, but even a book of memoirs written by an anonymous ex-prostitute would probably sell well. No one would wonder exactly who had written them.

Madame Kitten casually wondered who had sent her "Those Mysterious Signals from Space." It was actually from New York City. There was no message; the address was written in a hand Madame Kitten had never seen.

Then this invisible hand directed her to turn from the appealing blank space on the back to the glossy cover picture, with all its obvious symbols. In a corner of the chaotic design Madame Kitten suddenly discovered some tiny but readable words that formed a clear question.

Now Madame Kitten was not immune to the allure of the visual. But remember she was an ex-prostitute. She'd seen as many faces as bodies. Even the penis on the Venus did not surprise her. In her business she'd seen everything. They were no mysteries. But questions? Questions were the very essence of mystery.

This question was: When is it not wrong to just daydream?

(There were other words in the picture, but not all words are questions. Still, being interested in larger questions, Madame Kitten might have found a signal in the words "Demi Gods," written in an arc in the opposite corner. But nearby was a picture of a muscleman naked from the waist up. This happened to remind Madame Kitten too much of her ex-pimp.)

As Madame Kitten began wondering about this new question she stopped wondering who had sent her the postcard.

Madame Kitten, as an ex-prostitute, preferred ideas to people. Is this why she did not care who had sent her the postcard? Or are some questions just more interesting than others?

Do you wonder what daydream Madame Kitten had?
Or would you prefer to know what Madame Kitten looked
like?

It is all part of the same story: Madame Kitten wished
to escape the body of her past.

These days Madame Kitten worked in a perfume shop.
It was by taking this job that she had escaped her pimp.
(He never thought to look for her in a perfume shop.) But
her memories still—yes—haunted her.

Up to now Madame Kitten had tried to escape time by
visual means: art. The art of her *maquillage* was such that
at thirty years old, Madame Kitten usually looked either
girlish or middle-aged.

Looking ages not her own allowed Madame Kitten to
pretend her real past did not belong to her. It was easy for
her to look like a fresh-faced schoolgirl, so young and
fresh it was impossible that a dozen years ago she had
been a ripe-bodied whore with a blonde bouffant.

Turning this trick did not, in truth, always please
Madame Kitten. She sometimes liked remembering the
past—as long as it was not her own. So she often went to
considerably more effort, applying layers of pancake
makeup to hide lines that did not exist. In this mask
Madame Kitten did not have to entirely miss her past. She
could look back on her youth as if it were the youth of an
adored but wayward daughter.

Madame Kitten had never been a wayward daughter,
only a granddaughter following in the footsteps of her
grandmother Nana, who had raised her.

Fifty years ago, Nana had been a *nana*. This was a special type of prostitute popular among lovers of flesh of
those days. Those lovers—those butchers—sold tripe.
Nanas sold their overripe bodies. They were not only
floozies; they were fat.

Fat was more fashionable in those days than in Madame

Kitten's. One day Madame Kitten decided to slim down. Madame Kitten's decisions were always sudden, inspired only by mysterious signals. In this case it was a practical matter too; she was losing too many customers. So she ate like an ascetic. Soon her body reached the aesthetic. At the same time the bouffant too deflated to fashion.

Another day, just as suddenly and without any practical considerations whatever, Madame Kitten became an ex-prostitute and found employment in a perfume shop.

It was in the perfume shop that Madame Kitten learned the futility of her art.

It did not matter what she looked like, no matter how many mirrors she looked into; the essence of her past came floating back to her in invisible signals of scent.

She might have walked the streets, looking for another job, but it wouldn't have worked. The streets of Paris are known not only for their beauty but also for their pungent smells.

Madame Kitten had no signals for the future and no-where else to go—until the postcard appeared. The signal was given. Her future would take place in—must take place in—New York City.

(We know that Madame Kitten dreamed of worlds outside the one she lived in. So it should come as no surprise that she had learned a little English long ago.)

Thus Madame Kitten decided: The answer to the question "When is it not wrong to just daydream?" was "the past." Since it was now the present, she must stop daydreaming and go to the American embassy or consulate or both and get the necessary papers for her journey.

In the business of bureaucracy it may be impractical to just daydream, but it is impossible not to. Madame Kitten walked through official channels as if in a dream. She filled out innumerable forms with invisible hands.

At work she floated through her duties like a wraith,

195

daydreaming of the future instead of the past. Everyone found her charmingly romantic. Women who came to the shop for a mysterious essence to transcend physical love found Madame Kitten to be the very essence of that essence.

Should Madame Kitten have been practical as well as romantic? Should she have prepared for her entrance into modern American space by studying our scientific discoveries—e.g. space programs, Cape Canaveral, etc.? This scientific side of course also exists in France, but when one is a prostitute or perfume girl in Paris, technology does not play an important role in everyday life.

Nor does space technology play an important role in this story.

PART 2. NEW YORK

On paper, Madame Kitten could not lie. She could lie with makeup, she could lie with customers, but all those official papers bore the truth: Madame Kitten was her real name.

As soon as she got to New York Madame Kitten wished she had remembered her English better. Her name was the only part of her past that was still around to embarrass her.

Of course she'd discovered, long ago, what "kitten" meant in English, but in Paris she never had to think about it much. After all nobody called her Madame Le Chat. In fact for years nobody addressed her as Madame Kitten either. Since it was her real name she didn't use it. No Parisian prostitute was ever who she said she was. Madame Kitten had had as many false names as she had had johns. Unlike the other prostitutes, who took one false name and stuck to it, Madame Kitten did not want to become too well-known. In each new house or street she started fresh. Her pimp did not mind, because as a result she was always meeting new people, who often liked her well enough to find her in her new place. In fact the name of Madame Kitten was famous because she had so many aliases.

Madame Kitten thought she escaped her pimp by going back to using her real name, but she was wrong. It was just that the pimp never believed a prostitute had the power to become an ex-prostitute and so he never thought to look for her in a perfume shop.

Upon arrival in New York, Madame Kitten did not think to look for a job in a perfume shop. She could sense that perfumes are not big business in New York City.

Instead she got a job as a cleaning woman in a large office building in midtown, working the graveyard shift.

This schedule did not bother Madame Kitten since she was used to doing night work. Not that this routine of mopping and scrubbing much resembled her previous night work. It might have struck her as something cleaner and purer, but it didn't. Sometimes Madame Kitten was realistic: she recognized this for the drudgery it was. It was not the work itself but the space that fascinated her.

She worked in dark space that was not meant to be dark and so was mysterious.

And now that she was a stranger herself she did not have to meet any new strangers. Madame Kitten worked alone all night long.

For several months Madame Kitten performed her ablutions alone in the dark. One night she finally heard a voice calling to her.

It was another cleaning lady's.

Now Madame Kitten worked under fluorescent lights, alongside a black woman named Blanche. Blanche insisted on the lights. She'd been cleaning for ten years but still she couldn't do it with the lights off.

Blanche's sudden appearance in the office found Madame Kitten embarrassed all over again. She was forced to tell Blanche her name.

"Madame Kitty, eh?" said Blanche, who was slightly deaf. "Sounds like a French whore to me."

"Please, call me Madame K.," said Madame Kitten in a sudden inspiration.

"Call me Blanche," said Blanche.

Usually, however, they didn't call each other anything. There wasn't any need to. They were the only two in the place and anything said by one of them was obviously said to the other. Blanche was curiously uninterested in tales of Madame K.'s past or even of Paris. But she did want to know where Madame K. was sleeping these days.

"I have a little room in a residence hotel on 110th Street," Madame K. replied guardedly.

"You one of those people who always lives in hotels?" Blanche wanted to know.

"I'm staying there, yes," admitted Madame K. "Always. I don't want to move any longer."

Blanche considered. "They got some nice fruit-and-vegetable markets in that neighborhood," she said. "Open 24 hours. Lucky for those who work nights."

"I'm not interested very much in food," Madame K. said.

"Not interested in food? Who isn't interested in food?" laughed Blanche. "Can't afford not to be interested in food, you know. Food and a roof over your head's what you got to be interested in these days."

"I'm interested enough to get this job to pay for them," Madame K. admitted.

"Don't you know it," said Blanche. "You got any kids? I got two kids. They like to eat, too."

"No," said Madame K., "just me."

"Just you and me, babe," sang Blanche. "And who's got time for a love life with a job like this?"

The next day Madame K. went to a pet shop and bought a little kitten. On her way home she stopped in at one of the fruit-and-vegetable markets near her room and found that they also carried cat food. Since she did not know her kitten's taste, Madame K. bought every variety.

Soon the kitten was a fat cat, but Madame K. continued to call her Kitten. "Kitten has a great appetite," she told Blanche proudly.

Blanche, who was fat, reminded Madame K. of her Nana.

The two women dusted and scrubbed in companionable silence these days. There was not much new to talk about. Madame K. found herself daydreaming of her lost days of innocence. This was not very interesting, so she began thinking about the day they ended. It was when she discovered what it was her grandmother used to do.

Madame K. reflected: Everyone starts out with innocence and then loses it, but I might have been a perfume girl without a past if my grandmother had not been a *nana*.

The enormity of her Nana's reputation weighed heavily on Madame K.

One night Blanche disappeared as suddenly as she had appeared. Madame K. decided that Blanche had merely quit. Madame Kitten no longer believed in mysterious signals as much as she had in Paris. In formulating this theory of Blanche's absence Madame Kitten thought she was being quite realistic.

The real reason Blanche was no longer there was inflation. In New York City cleaning ladies cost more than whores.

Life was not the same immediately following Blanche's departure. Madame K. began talking to herself out loud.

"I miss Blanche, but now I can turn the lights out while I work," she announced.

After she had turned the lights off, Madame K. discovered she did not have much else to say to herself.

Madame K. realized her new life gave her nothing new to think about, but she was afraid to put this thought into words and so she kept quiet. Anyway she didn't have anybody to say it to.

Then she fell asleep.

After this, Madame K. often fell asleep on the job, but standards of cleanliness are not high in New York City and nobody seemed to notice the difference Madame K.'s nightly naps made.

Thus Madame K. was not in danger of losing her job. Nor was she in any other kind of danger from the outside world.

What can happen to Madame Kitten when she has a dream job, a roof over her head, and a fruit-and-vegetable market open 24 hours a day?

Nothing.

Naturally the last mysterious signal anybody gets in life is nothingness.

How could Madame K. know that New York City is just another symbol? In escaping her past did she lose her future? In Paris, there is always a past—there is always her past. But in New York? In New York the future is only a dream.

For cleaning ladies like Blanche, anyway.

If Madame Kitten *truly lives* only in the past, does this mean she will live forever? Will the fruits of her immorality be immortality?

Maybe if she writes her memoirs.

Remember that Madame K. has all but forgotten her past. She is now only haunted by her *Nana's* past. The ripe body of her own has shrunk in comparison.

But we are not just faces and bodies. We are also our Nanas and our Kittens. And Madame K.'s kitten is as fat as ever.

One night, while she is napping and dreaming, Madame

K. sleepwalks to one of the office typewriters and types out, in the first person, in French, the story of her Nana's life.

The next morning, the secretaries in the office discovered somebody had left some typed-up paper in the typewriter overnight.

This disarray did not surprise them because standards of neatness are only slightly higher than standards of cleanliness in this city.

One sharp-eyed girl did, however, realize that nobody in the office that they knew could have typed it because it seemed to be typed in something resembling French* and nobody that they knew knew much French.

Did this girl or any of her young, fresh-faced, slim-bodied American colleagues think this was a mysterious signal from space?

Of course not. In New York these days, young working girls are not on the lookout for mysteries, even when they are in English.

They are, however, on the lookout for a diet that really works.

PART 3. THE FUTURE

Meanwhile, Paris is still there. For every French person in New York, there are ten Americans in Paris. . . . Now it is time for one American man to stop daydreaming. The successful New York businessman who had anonymously sent Madame K. the mysterious postcard—an ex-john with a spiritual, if not ascetic, bent—returns to the Paris of his past. Some things are too good to forget. Paris, prostitutes, perfume. . . . He finds out she'd become a

*Madame K. had mis-typed several words, owing to some different places of French and American characters on the typewriter.

perfume girl. What the ex-pimp doesn't know, the ex-john discovers. Fate is on his side! He goes looking for the perfume girl/ex-prostitute of his past.

At every perfume shop, the ex-john, potential soul mate asks, "Where is she? Where is Madame Kitten?"

All over Paris, everyone who once knew her well, no matter what her name or weight or hairdo, everyone who could never forget her replies:

"Madame Kitten? It is a great mystery what has happened to her."

Los Angeles

_____

SHE IS one of Los Angeles—Los Angeles de Carlos. (TV Hispanica? No, just TV . . . it's the action that matters, not the language.) And the readers of the _Federal Enquirer,_ the _Hollywood Star,_ the _Midnight Rambler,_ the _Tittle-Tattler:_ they know everything about her, about how she hides away in her penthouse for privacy, against the dangers that lurk outside for one so beautiful and desirable. . . . This one, this Angeles—she is not their favorite. (There are 2 others, and one of them is Blonde.)

She is brunette, perfect of feature, with a high smooth forehead and high smooth cheekbones. She is also from Texas, where she got a God-fearing upbringing.

And now she is one of LOS ANGELES! Los Angeles de Carlos . . . the stupid one, they say, who never says anything, much.

(The Blonde is the most popular. There is always only one Blonde, and she is the most popular, always. Blonde No. 2 is "younger sis of Blonde No. 1." More wholesome, maybe. But still a Blonde.)

Week after week, Los Angeles get into trouble. They go looking for adventure, they play impossible roles, they are exposed, they escape death.

Do millions watch them only for their beauty? Or for their beauty, risked—

Calm down, calm down! Los Angeles are always calm, never any hysteria, never any tears—

Her name is Patricia, a cool name for a cool beauty, and she dreamed of what every little girl dreams of: soft silky love, Romance under the stars, that kiss that melts into . . . the end of the dream.

They don't teach Freud in Texas, she never knew that The Kiss meant something else, altogether.

This Patricia, she has ordinary dreams. She is not one of Los Angeles, in real life, she is always protesting to the interviewers from *TV Guide*. She disappoints, this Patricia.

But there is always the Blonde . . . (No. 1 or No. 2). When she runs, those long tresses flowing. . . .

See the Blonde, with her long tresses flowing as she runs. . . .

She is always the mystery. She changes from Blonde No. 1 to Blonde No. 2 as the TV seasons change. . . .

Nobody knows what the Blonde thinks. She thrusts a gleaming tanned hip out from life-size posters; the men stare, and stare, and stare. . . .

But Casting, where is the redhead?

Well, these are not times of absolute symmetry. Or, then again, allowing for omissions, they are.

O.K. Two brunettes and a Blonde, then. A Smart One, a Stupid One, and a Blonde.

It's not true, the Blonde protests, that no one knows what I think. It's in my eyes, on my Posters. And if you cannot discover anything there, there is always the *Tattler*, to tittle what they know.

So you are not a mysterious woman?

Naah. I am only a perfect woman. Anyone knows there is no mystery in that.

Who is Carlos?

Carlos is the mystery man. Nobody sees him, though that voice is familiar.

Poor Los Angeles de Carlos, they have everything except knowledge of who they are, who they belong to. . . .

See this! says Patricia's mother, to Patricia's father. Look at her on TV, making eyes, running away, lying to men. See this and weep, that this is our daughter.

Read this and rejoice, says Patricia's father, who happens to be a minister, pointing to a *TV Guide*. "An Old Fashioned Girl." This is who our daughter is. ". . . I am from Texas, and I fear God. . . ."

At last, it is Patricia's turn. Patricia is involved in a serious romance! When can we meet him? the others want to know.

—Drop by, take a look, turn green with envy.

Patricia smiles, so they know she is joking.

After the Blonde leaves, Patricia turns to her fellow brunette, confides that she is scared—it's all so new and exciting, it's all happening so fast—

—As long as you don't crash and burn. . . .

—That's not the plan.

—It never is.

The man Patricia has fallen for is a pilot. When he finds out that she is not ready to take off at a moment's notice, that in fact she is not the free-spirited girl she said she was, but rather a "trained private investigator"—

Los Angeles are hunting gangsters. Patricia and the Blonde are dispatched to Reno. The Smart One is sent to New York—it must be the Smart One who is sent to New York—

See the 747 whooshing through transcontinental space

. . . see the prop plane pleasure-hopping to Reno . . . in one sky in one day, 2 beautiful Angeles in one plane, 1 in a second. . . .

In New York, the Smart One changes from her customary striped turtleneck and "nice" pants into a business suit, complete with narrow skirt in the latest high-fashion style. As soon as she enters the mobster's office, secret alarms go off. Her gun has been detected! But after all, this is New York, sophisticated technology is routinely employed. . . . The Smart One keeps her cool as the mobster strips her of her gun. Honesty and a pretty face is the best policy.

—I'm a licensed private detective from the City of Angels.

—You've got spirit, I'll give you that.

Back at the New York hotel, the Smart One cleverly dodges a bullet and bolts into her room. The phone rings.

It's Patricia and the Blonde, calling from a poolside phone, wearing nothing but bikinis in the hot Reno sun.

—Hi, we've been trying to reach you, we're having a wonderful time. . . .

—Someone just took a shot at me.

—You be careful!

Interview with the Smart One:

Do you dream?
Yes, when I'm not on the set.
What are your dreams like?
My dreams are dangerous.
Do you act out your dreams?
Yes . . . in my dreams.
Not in your life?
Nobody does in their life.
But your life is acting. You can get into danger every week.

208

You mean Los Angeles.
You have adventures every week.
It's not the same.
Because you know they will always turn out all right?
Because I never feel them. The adventures.
Heartless unemotional intellectual bitch that you are—
No. But every time I start running, I have to stop. We all talk about it. The cameramen fiddle around. Then I start running again.
So you never get away.
I never even get excited!
You never have adventure.
And I want adventure.
Why don't you fly a plane?
Scares me too much.
Have an affair?
Scares me not enough. You know, it's the same old thing.
What do you do, to have fun?
Oh . . . I . . . watch TV.
What do you watch?
I watch Los Angeles de Carlos. I'm just like everyone else, you know. I like to watch beautiful girls get into trouble, and get out of it, and imagine that I'm one of those . . . strangers. . . .

Where is Carlos?
Los Angeles never see him. They are entrusted to his *agent d'affaires,* a middle-aged man with jowls, a jolly buffoon. Los Angeles laugh at their protector, tease him . . . he is no temptation. . . .
He has told them that Carlos is immensely rich, a play-boy of the grand manner, with blondes and brunettes at every appendage . . . a man of earthy pleasures, so satis-fied that he does not really desire the company of Los Angeles . . . not even the sight of Los Angeles. . . . They only hear him over the Intercom, making jokes, giving

orders, expressing concern for their safety, all in the most fatherly voice—but he won't let them see him—his magnificence might tempt them. . . .

An awful thought, that Los Angeles might be taken away from their lives of adventure, merely to grace one arm or the other of an irresistible playboy.

Still, Patricia yearns to see him. Every night as she sleeps she dreams of him, hears his voice . . . then it is only a leap of faith to imagine his arms. . . . She feels herself lifted far above her bed in the sweet penthouse. . . .

One starlit night in the City of Angels, home of Los Angeles. . . .

A man overlooks the vast freeways from a penthouse suite. He is guarding one of Los Angeles from her pursuers . . . he must . . . it is his job. But when she is almost asleep, he sneaks out like a cat burglar to the balcony and looks out over the City. Strings of cars sparkle at him. He closes his eyes and then opens them wider. He sees, in each car, a beautiful female thrill-seeker; and in each thrill-seeker, a beautiful female he might once have taken to bed. There have been so many. . . . A blonde here, a brunette there, and—yes—plenty of redheads, full of spark and fight—

This man of catholic taste marvels at the City stretched out underneath him, this Los Angeles of soft bodies in hard chrome cars. . . .

He is Boswell, and the Life of Los Angeles is in truth his life . . . all of it is his, Los Angeles, the City. . . . All of his dreams have come true—but only in secret: everyone thinks he belongs to Los Angeles, when it is just the reverse. . . . He only protects Los Angeles because he has created them. They are Boswell's Los Angeles. . . . They are his to give, his to take. . . . And they crave Carlos! But Carlos is only the pretender to the throne! Carlos too is his—he is Carlos! It is Boswell the eunuch servant of

Carlos who has conceived Los Angeles! Who possesses them! Who refuses to let them possess him because . . . there are so many others. . . . He is the true Carlos de Los Angeles, and he is the Boswell of the City. Soon it will be secret no longer—he will call reporters from the *Tattler*, the *Star*, the *Enquirer*—he will write his own story! He will tell them . . . that it all belongs to him: every twinkling car, every poolside chaise lounge, every beauty's blood and pulse. It all belongs to him, and yet— and still—something is missing . . . there is no adventure, nothing left to pursue, now that all his glittering dreams have come true. . . . There is no life for conquerors anymore, no dangers to defy. The only dangers belong to Los Angeles, his Los Angeles, and he can only protect them. . . .

Above the penthouse there are stars, and above the street there are streetlamps, burning hot and bright in the murky night air. It is said that there is not enough of something in the City of Angels this season, not enough—not enough water. . . . It is not known how long the City can bear it. Suddenly water is a precious commodity: ". . . Conservation is the weapon to fight the danger. . . ." But thirsts are growing more and more desperate. All over the City of Angels beautiful starlets are thinking for the first time— No water! How will I flush out the impurities of City air from my pores?

Patricia is lounging on her bed, surrounded by newspapers. Now she is drifting off, breathing softly into the pages of the *Rambler*. . . . This Patricia, she is too sleepy-headed to realize her danger; she dreams only about fans, paparazzi, crazy men who have threatened to shoot her, slash her, mutilate her perfect body—

The Death of Joe Dassin

PART I

L'ÉTÉ INDIEN

THE TIMING seemed perfect. It was fall, mid-September when I arrived in Paris for a stay of several months with my friend Usa, like me a New Yorker originally from the Midwest, but blonde. We were expecting warmth and that first week it was as warm as we could wish. It was Indian summer, *l'été Indien*—by coincidence, also the name of a song we'd heard just before crossing the Channel. A boy in London had played it for us, a love song crooned by a very famous French singer called Joe Dassin. I'd never heard of him. "Yes, he's very famous," Usa said knowledgeably, "a French version of Tom Jones." We listened to Joe sing about love, the past, and the beach, and other words in thrilling low whispers of French we couldn't make out. Usa and I agreed that Joe Dassin was very sexy, but not (like Tom Jones) just for housewives. Because he was French we forgave him his sentimentality.

The boy in London told us "L'Été Indien" was an old song—it had been a hit five years ago. But the song still seemed to be popular in Paris. We found it on almost every jukebox in every café in our quarter, the Latin.

We threw away lots of francs playing that song again and again.

213

Judy Lopatin

THE WEATHER IN THE LUXEMBOURG GARDENS

Though it was not exactly the right season, I was in the mood for everything that Paris in the spring is supposed to be.

Every day I walked up to the Luxembourg Gardens to sit in the sun and enjoy the flowers. Men appeared, most not my style, some interesting. A young doctor, born in Tunisia, very slick and Parisian, sat down close to me and delivered a lecture on genetic engineering and micro-biology, the latest advances in modern science. Surprisingly, I understood most of the technical terms. Science is now an international language, like love used to be. This doctor specialized in resuscitating dead bodies, or bodies nearly so, he told me. I nodded: I had heard many sirens in the streets of Paris, police cars or ambulances. Did he work in an emergency ward? No, he explained, he was more important than that: he received the victims after the emergency ward could do nothing. He told me about drugs I'd never heard of and then invited me for a drink, expecting that I would follow him immediately. But it was still warm in the gardens and I wanted to stay and see what else might happen. When I wondered aloud, and in French, why an important doctor had to pick up American girls in the Luxembourg Gardens, he got very insulted and informed me that all the women in the hospital chased after him.

Soon after he stalked off I felt the wind change. It was getting colder. Nothing else had changed, just the weather. It was time to leave the gardens and go sit in a café.

PARADISE

Do passions change with the weather? Not the passions of the men of Paris, who will follow any woman down the street for blocks trying to seduce her. The Latin Quarter

214

in particular is a paradise for men from foreign parts looking for likely women to seduce, young students or tourists
preferred.

Summer in New York had been very hot. French boys,
tourists in America, most of them students, appeared
wherever I went. One of them, Laurent, warned me,
"Paris is not paradise." He was young and appealing but
overly serious, a pessimist about his countrymen. He
painted a picture of Paris as a city of cheats and con-men,
then tried to kiss me. Since all his arguments had been
political, I saw no bad timing or faulty logic in this move.
But his kisses were wet and sloppy.

As the weather got colder in Paris that fall, I wondered
if I had missed something in Laurent's warning about the
morals of the Parisians. I was not out on the streets much,
preferring to find a café that kept its doors closed, but as I
rushed down the streets of the Latin Quarter looking for
warmth strange and ugly men pursued me. My light
gabardine jacket was no protection. When my pursuers
tried to strike up a flirtation, I complained about the
weather. *"Il n'y a plus de saisons à Paris,"* one man replied. I told him he was wrong. Hadn't it been warm,
Indian summer, just a week ago?

"Dégage," I finally said, to get rid of him. It was a
word Laurent had taught me. I thought it meant go away
but it seemed to mean something far worse. *"Ce n'est pas
joli, ça,"* the man said, but now thinking me ugly, he did
go away.

HISTORY

Paris in the—

What is Paris without a past? Somewhere in France, I
knew, there was a boy with exactly as long a past as I. We
met on my first visit to Paris, a year ago, in—

—the spring, at a street fair in a very old quarter of
Paris called Le Marais. I was a tourist then—wanting to

see Paris, not meet Frenchmen—and my guidebook advised an exploration of Le Marais's old Jewish streets. But that evening Le Marais was hosting a street fair, and the mood, while foreign to the average Frenchman, was not Israelite (what the French call Jewish), but Italian. I wandered into a crowd watching a commedia dell'arte play, and after the farce was over I met Philippe, the boy whose birthday matched mine.

To Philippe, who was studying the stars with a fervor that only the French are capable of these days, this meant we were meant to meet. But we both had our own reasons for being in Le Marais in the first place; Philippe was half-Italian. He was also pretty, which is why I happened to pick him up.

When we discovered our connection, I tried to think of him as what I might be if I had been born a man in France of Italian extraction, though we looked nothing alike. He was blond, with slightly primitive features in a face that was mysteriously pretty, playful, even girlish. But maybe this was something about Philippe that had nothing to do with his features, because he looked the same way faceless. Before I saw that pretty-primitive face in the crowd, I saw just the back of his head, and another young man's hand tousling Philippe's wild blond hair, and then that hand resting casually on Philippe's shoulder. From a distance and before he turned around, I thought Philippe might be a woman. But this first impression was forgotten until several weeks later when I spent a weekend at the house these two young men shared in the countryside.

Since then I had written once or twice to Philippe, and he had sent me a birthday card and one letter, in which he announced that Paul, his lover, had committed suicide, and everything had changed.

For the first week after Usa and I arrived in Paris, those days of Indian summer, I thought about Philippe and his sad history as if he were still in a foreign country. But when I realized our twenty-sixth birthday was only a couple of weeks away, I decided it was important to renew our connection in the flesh.

A HIGH POINT

Night after night in the cafés we sat and watched Paris pass us by. Everybody looked very modern, except the café waiters, who reminded me of the French Revolution.

One evening at a café on the Boulevard St. Germain a young lawyer in a well-cut suit picked us up and drove us home in his sports car. Usa and I sat in the back on either side of a baby's car seat. The next night we sat in a different café next to two boys with fresh faces like schoolboys and picked them up.

One of them, Michel, was a schoolboy—studying philosophy at a university on the fringes of Paris, and writing a book whose hero was a 10-franc bank note. He was a quiet type with soft, velvety eyes and rotten teeth. At the time I didn't notice the warts on his fingers. The other boy, Hervé, was an ambulance driver with a cherubic face and an overgrown Beatle haircut. He seemed to be one of the most good-natured people I had ever met, always laughing, not maniacally but from real joie de vivre. The boys had been buddies in Berlin, in the French army.

I was surprised to hear that the French army was still stationed in Berlin. I said to Michel, "Look at that waiter. Doesn't he look like somebody from the French Revolution?" But Michel did not understand what I was talking about, and I could not explain, since I knew nothing about the French Revolution. A few moments later I asked Michel about his family and he revealed that his mother had been, before her marriage, a laundress. I thought of Zola and cast the French Revolution waiter in his white smock as a baker.

But the waiters of Paris are far too haughty to consider

themselves workers of any present or historical sort. Our baker ordered us to order more drinks or leave the café. "There's nothing here anyway," the boys said with bravado, "let's drive up to Montmartre."

Though it was just after midnight all the cafés of the Place du Tertre were closed. The four of us stood in the deserted square and looked down on the city of Paris. I hoped Michel would kiss me, despite his rotten teeth, but he was too polite, or too young, to do so. We found an old telescope and all looked down at Paris through that. I asked, "Is this the highest point in Paris?" Not anymore, the boys said, now it was the Tour Montparnasse—the highest skyscraper in Paris.

THE EFFICIENCY OF THE POLICE

The cold weather began to force us to retreat inside the cafés. But some people, Americans mostly, still sat outside on the *terrasses* and pretended it was a lovely foreign night.

One of these nights, a wild savage, big and burly and bearded, appeared out of nowhere to terrorize these terrace-sitting tourists in three or four fashionable cafés on the Boulevard St. Germain.

I was drinking my *café crème* inside, away from any real danger, but at the sound of the commotion I hurried out into the street. (Usa was in the *lavabo,* fixing her makeup.) At first I thought the wild man might be another one of those peculiar Parisian café entertainments, like mimes and fire-eaters, but he wasn't wearing the right costume—though it would have been too cold for loincloths in any case.

I saw the wild man laugh and tables collapse, and I kept my distance. But when the wild man reeled down the street and the tourists righted their tables, I looked at their laps to see what they'd been drinking.

218

Moments later I heard police sirens. The wild man, oblivious of the consequences of his crimes, was destroying the next café in his path. As the sounds of sirens in the streets are always present in Paris, I waited until I saw the police in the flesh before I felt any real relief. They arrived in large numbers, at least fifteen short, sharp French uniforms, captured the wild man quickly, and shoved him into a police-van.

Just as the excitement was over, Usa came back from the *lavabo*. I told her what she had missed. "The poor man," she said. I described the spectacle again, how scary it had been.

Not having witnessed the scene, she cursed the efficiency of the police.

PART II

GARBAGE

The first day of October it was suddenly winter. Nobody could pretend it was warm anymore. Parisians who seemed to have loafed all day long at the cafés got down to business. Construction workers drilled the sidewalks of the fashionable Opera area on the Right Bank—a haunt of mine for its Monoprix dime store and the mail service at American Express—probably to beautify Paris for its next Spring.

In the meantime, there was no heat in our hotel—because our room was too cheap, we thought. But we were too poor, too lazy, too cold to think of looking for another place. We complained to our *patron* instead. He laughed—he was used to indigent American adventurers, he made his living from them—and blamed the City of Paris. Our hotel, he claimed, was heated by city garbage—whatever the people of Paris happened to throw away on any given day.

219

We thought he was joking—our *patron* seemed a good-natured sort, if not a jokester—but he repeated his story and stuck to it.

Paris cannot be nearly as clean a city as its reputation for beauty suggests. The Parisian population on the whole looks remarkably well-fed and well-dressed, and prosperous people create a lot of garbage. However, it is true that there is less garbage floating about its streets than those of New York or Rome. Since we knew all this potential garbage was not being burned, it had to be somehow hidden.

Paris, I decided, must be full of hoarded garbage.

THE FRENCH SYSTEM

For a few days it was too cold to wash my hair (the water too was heated, or not, by garbage) and I didn't feel pretty enough to go out to a café. Instead I tried drinking a bottle of cheap wine in my hotel room—not exactly secret drinking since Usa was doing the same thing. Even though we knew it was an illusion we began to feel warmer. But the warmer I got, the more I wondered about Philippe and why he had never returned a message I left with a woman living in his house in the country. So with unwashed, unkempt hair, I went to a café and was picked up by two coiffeurs from Alsace, who were in town to learn the latest haircutting techniques from Vidal Sassoon.

Slick men with well-groomed moustaches were not my type, but I let them buy me a drink. The younger one, baptized Johnny by a father who had met American Johnnys during World War II, picked up the strands of my hair with practiced fingers and counseled a good cut. Then, as if by prearrangement, he lost interest and left me to the attentions of his companion, a middle-aged man who drew me diagrams of some French system of occult metaphysics. I had no idea what he was talking about. "Okay," he said finally, "take this." It was a hot-pink business card, Coiffures by Jean-Pierre. "In case you find yourself in Alsace and need a friend." He grabbed me around my throat in an amorous choke. When I pushed him away his cigarette left a little red mark on my arm I knew would never go away.

I felt sad that I was permanently disfigured by a hairdresser who meant nothing to me.

TROUBLES IN PARIS

The next morning there was trouble. We woke to the sound of a sudden snap, a squeal that wasn't human. With dead certainty I announced, "It's the mouse." Usa bravely got up, looked at the trap, and squealed too—not as high-pitched as the mouse's. She had first sighted it, alive, one night when I was out at a café, and though it had disappeared to some hiding-place by the time I got home, we had the *patron* set a trap anyway. The *patron* had several mousetraps on hand. We asked if there were mice in all the rooms. "*Il y a un ou deux qui se promènent dans la maison,*" he had admitted cheerfully. We laughed at the idea of mice promenading themselves.

Now the *patron* was delighted to hear that there was a dead mouse in our room.

To give new life and body to my hair, according to the instructions of Johnny and Jean-Pierre, I bought a bottle of *volume* shampoo in the Galeries Lafayette, then a round of Camembert in the Monoprix supermarket. These errands made me feel French. I pictured myself as a chic Parisian housewife, dedicated to beauty and food. I hoped the guillotined mouse would be gone when I got home.

On the street I passed a demolition project. To get away from the smoke I took refuge in a newsstand and scanned the magazine covers. Most of the names and faces were unfamiliar—movie stars or politicians? I wondered. It oc-

221

curred to me that I didn't even know what Joe Dassin looked like. Then, suddenly, there he was—or his name, in a headline on *Paris Match*. But the cover picture was a photo of an ordinary-looking woman, a blonde, and the headline said, "*La veuve de Joe Dassin crie, On m'a volé mes enfants!*" I stared at the cover a few moments before I could translate it, and then I was confused. If *veuve* meant widow, could Joe Dassin be dead? If he was dead, who was stealing his children, and why?

"He is gone, *le petit souri*," the *patron* told me when I returned from my errands. "*Le chat* is now having a very nice dinner." I went up to my room, relieved and ready to collapse, only to find the Spanish maid cleaning the sink with the windows wide open for fresh air. Usa and I had decided to keep the windows forever shut and had tacked up a note in French saying so. But perhaps the maid did not understand our bad French. Though she spoke bad French too, hers was with a Spanish accent—according to Usa, who had already met the maid and had several difficult conversations with her.

I said *bonjour* and closed the window. The maid finished cleaning the sink and then closed the door so that the *patron* wouldn't see us. We sat down for a long chat.

Finally I began to understand: the maid, being Spanish, pregnant, and poor, had many troubles in Paris.

BAD TIMING

One day—a few days before our birthday—Philippe appeared in Paris to take me to lunch. Actually he had other business in the city; he and his mistress Elisabeth were setting up a bureau where they planned to give psychological-astrological consultations.

I was disappointed to hear about Elisabeth, but not really surprised that Philippe now had a mistress. Despite Paul he had always had several girlfriends. The weekend I

222

had visited the country house (formerly the village pres-
bytery, now the village scandal), many of the other female
guests had also had "histories" (*histoires*, what the French
call affairs) with Philippe, and one, possibly an ex-
girlfriend, had paraded about in her underwear. There
were also several children present, Paul's little boy and
three other little boys, all illegitimate, belonging to the
visitors. That night Philippe slept in the chapel with the
children.

"I wanted to sleep with you," Philippe assured me the
next day, "but right now it is too complicated." I remarked sadly that I was leaving soon, there was no time
left. "You Americans are always in a hurry for things to
happen," Philippe said. "When are you coming back to
France?" "Maybe never," I said.

Philippe had changed since Paul's suicide, I thought,
and told him so. His blond hair looked dirty, but he said it
was just its natural color in the fall, with no sun to bleach
it. He looked older, more than a year older. His sufferings
had, in addition to driving him further and further into
astrology, transformed his previously sunny outlook into
one of cynicism and practical egoism. I told him so. But
he was still nice enough not to tell me I looked older too.

I waited for the right moment to bring up Paul. But
Philippe calmly told me the story: Paul had been playing
his accordion in his room. His window was open. Neighbors in the village heard the music, and then suddenly the
music stopped. The next moment Paul threw himself out
the window.

"That's what the neighbor told me," Philippe added. "I
was in Italy with Elisabeth when it happened." "Did he do
it because you left him?" I asked delicately. "Not really,"
Philippe said. "I was already living with Elisabeth, I'd left
Paul long ago."

I made Philippe promise to try to slip away from Elisabeth on Sunday night so we could celebrate our birthday

together. He proposed that Elisabeth join us—she was eager to meet me and study my chart—and could not understand why I preferred to pretend that Elisabeth did not exist.

In my hotel room we rolled around on the bed kissing until Usa came in to change her clothes.

How different Philippe and I are, I thought, and what bad timing.

FRENCH HEROES

The next night, on a date with Hervé and Michel, I remembered to ask them if Joe Dassin was dead.

Hervé was driving us crazily through the streets of Paris to a little café he knew in the 16th *arrondissement*. Why this particular café, I wondered, when every café is more or less the same? But I didn't ask any questions, because I was sulking in the back seat. Usa had stayed home to wash her hair; she found understanding the boys' French, like the maid's, a chore. Her absence seemed to disappoint Michel, who informed me that she had beautiful eyes.

I resolved to pay most of my attention to Hervé, who was just as charming as Michel but had no warts on his fingers. Hervé was so lively that night that even his tape deck did not depress him. It was playing a sepulchral song called "Heroin" by Lou Reed, who had once been my hero.

"Ours too," the boys said. They told me they had seen him perform in Berlin and the talk led to more tales of army life. Despite the drills and the regulation crew cuts the boys had had a high time in Berlin. I wondered if that was where Hervé had learned ambulance-driving.

"Do you always drive your ambulance like this?" I asked Hervé as we narrowly missed cracking up, somewhere near the Opera. "The poor victims!" He laughed. "Usually I get them to the hospital before they die."

The Death of Joe Dassin

It was then that I remembered the mystery of the *Paris Match* cover story. "Is Joe Dassin dead?" I asked the boys.

"Sure," they said matter-of-factly. They were surprised I had heard of Joe Dassin and joked about his fans. "He's not one of our heroes," Hervé added. "But 'L'Été Indien' is a good song," I said, as though this were a joke too.

"You've fallen in love with a dead man," Hervé said, and we all laughed. They told me the story: Joe Dassin, age forty, had died only a few months ago, in Tahiti, of a *coronaire*—a heart attack, I guessed.

But I forgot all about asking why somebody was trying to steal his widow's children.

The café in the 16th *arrondissement* was as ordinary as I'd expected: another working-class bar with three or four pinball machines, typically Parisian. But as soon as we ordered our drinks Hervé was up in a flash to the phone booth and then, after a quick see-you-soon, out the door. Reluctantly I turned my attention back to Michel.

"He's going to visit a friend," Michel explained, "he'll be back soon." I thought about short visits in the middle of nowhere and said jokingly, "Drugs?" "Ssh," Michel said in a stage whisper that wasn't supposed to be funny.

It was then that I began to suspect Hervé's drug was, coincidentally, heroin. I whispered back to Michel—the word was the same in French—and he nodded sadly.

"But I only do it occasionally," Hervé told me laughingly when we were back in the car headed for the Latin Quarter. "And Michel is mistaken. Tonight I wasn't buying anything, I really did go to see my friend, to say goodbye. Tomorrow he is leaving on vacation."

We went to another café, exactly the same as the first but in my neighborhood. I felt safer. We didn't talk about heroin again. Instead, inspired by talk of our heroes, the boys and I quizzed each other about our favorite pop singers and actors, French and American, most of them alive.

Judy Lopatin

NEW PERFUME

The day before my birthday, wandering in the Galeries Lafayette, I succumbed to a sales pitch and bought a flask of Brigitte Bardot's new perfume.

Brigitte Bardot had never been my heroine but once I read in a magazine that she shared my sign. La Balance. Her perfume was called La Madrague and was supposed to smell of the sun, sand, and sea. Blow-ups of Brigitte, bleached and bronzed, hung over the perfume counters. I have never lived near the sea and look nothing like Brigitte, but I let the salesgirl spray me all over with the stuff—some French treatment of total immersion. Then I read the pamphlets: La Madrague was not just sun and sand, but the essence of irresistibility. Men who found themselves in its midst would be drawn irresistibly to its warmth.

I could not resist buying myself a birthday present. I walked out into the cold Paris afternoon smelling of the beach and wondered if all that Brigitte promised was true, if this breath of nature would truly startle the crowd, make passersby stop dead in their tracks.

Passersby were killed that morning on a street in the eastern section of Paris when a bomb exploded outside a synagogue. Like most Parisians, I was nowhere near the scene of the crime and only read about it in the papers later that day.

All evening I felt a vague sense of foreboding. Something wrong, I felt sure, was going to happen. Or had it already? I picked up my birthday present and played with the box. I wondered, Did I choose the wrong perfume?

A NORMAL EXPLOSION

A few hours later that same night—the early hours of Sunday, my birthday—our hotel room shuddered

226

and rocked with a terrible noise. We screamed, but it was already over. "It sounded like a bomb," Usa said. We went over to the window and looked out on the street and saw nothing. "Just a normal explosion," I said hopefully.

Sunday evening we had a party: Usa and I, and her New York boyfriend, who had just arrived in Paris. He brought some Dutch gin and we bought, instead of a birthday cake, some French pastries that were too sweet to eat. We admired them from afar and got drunk on the gin and waited for Philippe to call. He never did. "What this party needs is music," Usa said. "Why did we forget to bring a radio?" "We could go to a café and listen to the jukebox," I suggested. But at midnight Usa and her boyfriend went off to sleep together, and against their advice I went out alone to a café. I sat outside on the terrace in the cold air until my drunkenness wore off, and decided the day was over, nothing could get worse. Then I drank my *kir* very quickly and left the café.

On the street a man from Senegal approached me and invited me for a coffee. On an impulse I agreed. We went to another café. He asked me what was wrong and I recited my troubles. They sounded silly, but he took them seriously. "You must try to be happy," he said. "Life is composed of moments in the present."

I laughed. "You are very *gentille*," he added. I began to feel happier. He continued to analyze my character. "You try to be tough but you are not." Then, unexpectedly, he said, "Are you German? You look German." "Not at all," I said. "But you look like Nina Hagen. The punk singer. You know her?" "My traveling companion likes her, she plays her songs on the jukebox," I said. We didn't play Joe Dassin much anymore. "But I thought Nina Hagen was Dutch." "No, it's her boyfriend that's Dutch," the Senegalese said. "Do you want to go dancing?"

227

The next day I spent wandering around the city by myself. There seemed to be a sudden wave of Dutch people on holiday. Some of them were probably Germans, but I could hardly tell the difference and so I thought of all of them as Dutch.

Usa's boyfriend had just come from Amsterdam. Paris was the second stop on his European jaunt; he was just passing through on his way to London. But in the meantime, he planned to stay several days and make Usa fall in love with him.

When I returned to the hotel, I was afraid I might walk in on them, but the room was empty. I had nothing to do, so I read a book and waited half an hour before they got back. Usa's boyfriend announced that he had succeeded in procuring a room on the top floor of our hotel. We all agreed that this was more convenient than having to bribe the night porter at the hotel he'd been staying at to let Usa go upstairs after hours. "By the way," Usa said, "while you were out Philippe called and left a message. Last night he was sitting in his car in a traffic jam on the way into Paris, or he had car trouble, or both. Do you believe him?" "Both stories can't be true," I said crossly, "which was it?" "I'm not sure, it was hard understanding him," Usa said.

Usa's boyfriend tried to cheer me up. He waved the *Herald Tribune* at me and explained what had happened the night our hotel room had rocked with the terrible noise. It had in fact been a bomb, and a Dutchwoman—on holiday with her husband, whose birthday they were celebrating—had lost both her legs.

"The police think it's the fascists again," Usa's boyfriend went on, "it came just half a day after the synagogue bombing."

"Oh, was that the same day?" I said, surprised.

228

The Death of Joe Dassin

HOME

We decided to walk down the Boulevard St. Germain and survey the scene. There was not much visible damage; only one café's windows were boarded over. The bomb had gone off in the Dutchwoman's car, parked across the street. It was only a block or so away from our hotel, but on the dark side, the side our window did not look out upon.

I read the papers avidly for news of Mrs. Van P.'s condition. There was no change: she would never walk again; her legs were blown away. And her history: she was Dutch and not Jewish and did not know why this should happen to her.

The Latin Quarter, once menacing only for its ordinary men, seemed suddenly full of hidden fascists. I wondered if they could tell I was Jewish, then reminded myself that Mrs. Van P. was only an ordinary tourist on holiday.

Michel called that afternoon from his parents' house in the suburbs. As always, we had trouble understanding each other on the phone. There were long pauses. Finally he asked why I seemed to be feeling low. It occurred to me that Michel knew nothing about me, and I knew nothing about his family history—except that his mother was an ex-washerwoman. "The fascism," I said vaguely. "Yes, it's terrible," he said in a sympathetic tone. I wondered if we were talking about the same thing, the bomb set off at the synagogue, or some more abstract French concept. But I decided it was too hard to talk about in French on the phone.

Instead I told him about Mrs. Van P., the bomb in the car, the explosion and the tragedy—they were all easy words. This bomb, I told Michel, was too close to home.

229

PART III

A TRUE TRAGEDY

In time the true story of how Mrs. Van P. lost her legs appeared in the newspapers, shedding a new light on the tragedy.

One cold Saturday night, Mr. and Mrs. Van P., two Hollanders on holiday, sat in a café, celebrating Mr. Van P.'s birthday—perhaps celebrating being in Paris too. There being little to do in such a café celebration but drink, Mrs. Van P. was probably sinking into a warm pleasant stupor when her husband excused himself to "check something in the car" (Dutch people often drive to Paris). Soon he returned and they had one more nightcap.

As they strolled down the boulevard to their car, Mr. Van P. suddenly exclaimed that he wanted to take in more of the cold fresh air. Go ahead to the car, he told his wife, I'll walk a few blocks and you can pick me up down the street.

Mrs. Van P. amiably agreed, trotted off alone to the car, put the key in the ignition. Then she exploded.

As I had been haunted not so much by Mrs. Van P.'s leglessness as the causes behind it, I was now able to forget her tragedy. Husbands attempting to murder their wives is, after all, an everyday occurrence. The Paris police, checking into the history of Mr. Van P. in Holland, found him to be highly suspect not only with the Dutch authorities but also among his neighbors. A theory was advanced that, despite the overwhelming evidence, Mr. Van P. did not plant the bomb himself but was actually being framed by his enemies, also Dutch criminal types who might have holidayed in Paris that fateful weekend. As for the bomb, it was just a coincidence, or perhaps a sudden inspiration.

In the hospital, Mrs. Van P. held a press party and declared that she still believed in the innocence of her husband.

THE LIFE OF JOE DASSIN

There was one mystery of love that had not yet been solved. Joe Dassin was dead, his widow was the cover girl of *Paris Match*, but who was trying to steal their children? I bought *Paris Match* to find out.

The widow of Joe Dassin poured her heart out. Christine told *Paris Match* this story: her children had been kidnapped, purely and simply, by Joe's mother, who hated her—for stealing Joe, for not being Jewish. *"Cette dernière chose, elle me la reprochait d'une manière fanatique, avec des mots terribles. . . ."* The mother-in-law accused Christine of many crimes, of being sick, crazy, dangerous, anti-Semitic—*"oui, oui, moi, antisémite,"* Christine cried in indignation—she who had married Joe Dassin and had his children.

But this story, it seemed, was sad from the beginning. For seven years, as the mistress of a married man who also happened to be the heartthrob of France, Christine had suffered. And then, only two years after Joe finally married her, he asked for a divorce. This happened (Christine revealed dramatically) just one day after the birth of their second son. What horrible timing, I thought, but Christine claimed it was the work of the devil (Joe's mother). Or did she just not wish to speak ill of the dead?

I listened again to "L'Été Indien" and made out a few lines: Indian summer, sang Joe, is a season that exists only in North America. But still I knew nothing about Joe's real life, so I bought a fan magazine called *HIT*, a special issue devoted to Joe Dassin. On the first page I was surprised to see a photo of Joe smiling against the backdrop of a huge American flag, and the words: *"Joe,*

231

l'Americain qui se disait avant tout Parisien. . . ." Was it
true? In *HIT's* exclusive interview, Joe was asked if he felt
himself to be French or American.

American by passport, Joe said, French in his heart.

A PARTY

A German artist who knew somebody I knew in New
York invited Usa, her boyfriend, and me to a party. "Nobody has parties in Paris anymore because the junkies
steal everything," the German artist said, "but I have
nothing here to steal." The party was held in a bare sculp-
ture studio borrowed for the occasion. It was concrete and
cold until the *invités* arrived and began dancing up a
sweat to beach-party music. It was fast music, nothing
like Joe Dassin's beach or Brigitte's. It felt like New York.
For a while I forgot I was in Paris, the scene seemed so
familiar.

I met American models too dark or exotic to work in
America—"but now even in Europe they want the blonde
blue-eyed type"—German friends of the host in town for
the party, French people of various artistic occupations. I
got very drunk and looked around for somebody to kiss.
By chance the boy I picked was German, though in this
international crowd he looked merely international.
Claiming he was not a romantic type, he played very hard
to get. I told him I was Jewish to see what he would say.
He said, "You like me because you think I am a Nazi."
Then he smiled warmly.

I wandered off and found somebody else to talk to, this
time a Frenchman, another Philippe. It was my second or
third Philippe of the evening; I had never before realized
how common they were in France. This one made movies,
or rather one movie—a love story he could not finish

because the love affair was never over. "It's bad, but I cannot end it," he said. At the end of the party he took my hand, kissed it, and said, "Someday. . . ." His voice was musical, his hand was warm. For a moment my heart stopped. Then, with a shiver, I remembered where I was.

Fast and Loose, A Historical Romance

HE DEDICATED his life to brilliance and died of bad oysters.

This is the romance of Raymond Radiguet, whom Cocteau loved, whose heart was so hard Cocteau said you needed a diamond to scratch it.

Before Cocteau Raymond lived in a dream, in a suburban childhood he was eager to escape.

This teenage prodigy came to Paris on the eve of the decade of youth and love. He grew up so fast he died before youth had a chance to come into its vogue.

Did you discover love, Raymond Radiguet?

1921

At a ball among the smart set. . . .

Charming paper lanterns shimmer all around Raymond. It is the fashion to be à la Chinoise. . . . Under one lantern's glow, on the pavilion, is a woman in diaphanous white.

With surprise Raymond recognizes her from across the room. At such a distance she appears as remote and lovely as when he first saw her.

A week ago, a month ago—time has flown by— Raymond had visited an opium den. Few knew of this in

Paris. It was whispered about only in the most underground circles. Cocteau, who knew everybody, knew nothing about it. Cocteau would have nothing to do with opium. It was not his style. Nor did he wish it to be Raymond's. In this case, he was ignorant of the plot and therefore powerless. Raymond pleaded stomach-ache one night and left Cocteau. As arranged beforehand he met up with Brancusi, the sculptor, a man who liked to introduce young people to new things.

Raymond went to the opium den only as a spectator. He told himself that he was remaining faithful to Cocteau, in remaining faithful to his prejudices. But Raymond knew that this was not the fidelity Cocteau demanded. The fact that Raymond sought any pleasure without Cocteau's company was proof enough of his treachery.

It did not matter that Brancusi did not care for boys.

Raymond and Brancusi conspired that Cocteau should know nothing of this secret expedition. They arrived at a late hour when all were overcome by the languor of the opiate and oblivious of any newcomers.

The room was very dark. At first Raymond could see nothing but smoky vapors rising from corners of the room. Crouching in front of a low table, Raymond heard murmurings, muffled laughter that might have been sighs. . . . He thought of Cocteau. He felt Cocteau's invisible presence, felt him pressing against him so heavily he could not breathe.

Raymond was breathless. He opened his eyes and stared into the darkness. He could see nothing. But the air was heavy with scent . . . the scent of the laudanum, the perfume of a woman? Raymond could not tell which. The smells mingled in his nostrils, heavy and Oriental. Even as a spectator he began to feel faintly intoxicated.

Suddenly he found himself transfixed by the shadow before him. His eyes were now accustomed to the darkness. The shadow assumed human form; a woman's form. It was a woman on a divan—a throat choked in feathers, legs bound by fishnet, eyes— Her eyes looked as if consumed by dry ice. Then she closed them, and Raymond gazed at her face in its drugged repose. He thought: She is oblivious of her bondage.

He could not decide if he admired that or rather felt contempt.

Raymond's heart burned. He longed to reach out and touch her pale face. He was overcome with desire. Her invisible transports into death terrified him.

He rushed back to Cocteau at dawn with a recovered stomach and was for once grateful.

But now fate had arranged this second meeting with the woman, one far removed from the mysteries of that laudanum-scented night. . . . This time she was dressed like a shepherdess of another century (the eighteenth, perhaps), though it was not a costume-ball.

Raymond went up to speak to her, to see if she had really returned to the world.

'*Vous êtes habillée complètement différemment,*' he said to her.*

She had no idea what he was talking about and fell madly in love with him at once.

Raymond was not a handsome boy, but his soft milky skin and his childishly changeable features appealed to women. It was not until later that they discovered his cold heart, and at that instant their own hearts were captured completely.

Although she was already in love the woman had not yet made this discovery. She did not understand that Raymond was not like other men. His remark was not in the least an attempt to seduce her. Women ran after him; he did not need to court them.

* 'You are dressed completely differently,' *il lui a dit.*

Raymond did not appreciate the woman's English-shepherdess costume. He had compared it to her opium-den attire with disappointment.

The woman understood neither his disappointment nor the comparison. The night of her opium trance was not fresh in her memory. She usually wore white dresses of the shepherdess style. The only difference was that at times she also wore large hats with ribbons and carried baskets of live ducks to complete the look.

But at this ball she was not feeling her most theatrical.

'I don't think we have met,' the woman said, 'although of course I have heard . . . many things about you.'

Raymond took this as a compliment, and bowed with the exaggerated politeness he had recently adopted for women. From the corner of his eye he caught a glimpse of Cocteau, watching them with a vague and hateful smile.

Raymond turned to meet Cocteau's eyes with cold challenge in his own.

The woman's eyes followed Raymond's. She was fascinated with this young boy. Her heart was prepared to follow in Raymond's every path and share in his every emotion.

She did not realize that Raymond possessed but few emotions.

Cocteau turned away, anxious that he not appear too anxious.

Suddenly it was as if the man and the woman were completely alone. They suffered this lack of drama in a moment's pain. Raymond had had much practice at being cruel but often with an unknown woman he found himself not knowing what to say.

He was, despite all, only eighteen.

The woman decided to speak of her passion. She was a woman who understood its darker powers, its darker moments. Her name was Beatrice Hastings. She had been the mistress of the painter Modigliani and had exhausted herself in his violence. Since she had left him love was no less passionate for her, but she had learned to cloak this in conversation. She felt that Raymond would find the idea of love attractive only in its light moments, in creating light moments.

She was a dangerous woman who specialized in brilliant conversation.

'Are you in love?' Beatrice asked, with a curl of the lip that, while charming, betrayed the depth of her feelings.

Raymond was not surprised by her question, indeed a little bored. At such balls this seemed to be the question preying on the minds of all, absorbing every moment into a speculation of the past, a promise of the future. . . . Love affairs routinely excite interest, but Raymond's own affairs drew perhaps more than their share of attention. Many believed this due to the figure of Cocteau in the background. Because Cocteau was a *personnage* he and his affairs always assumed the foreground.

Raymond of course was well on his way to becoming a *personnage* in his own right. Therefore he was entitled to think that he alone inspired the curiosity. He was also well aware of his attractiveness to women. If the curious inquiry happened to come from a woman, Raymond believed there was something more than idle speculation, or even admiration. . . .

Nevertheless, his position in society demanded the form of fidelity. Not for the first time, Raymond was sorry to give his rehearsed response. 'I am loved,' he said, 'and that entails certain responsibilities as well as privileges.'

His air was both apologetic and warning.

The woman appeared satisfied by his answer. Raymond thought: 'She knows she might have me, if she is careful.'

He was only curious to see how she might proceed. Already he was thinking of her as he thought of all women. She was merely another. The power of the woman on the divan seemed far away.

239

They danced on the pavilion. Raymond closed his eyes, remembering her body in repose. He began dancing slower and slower. The undulations of her hips against him irritated him. His hands closed powerfully around her ribs and all but paralyzed her.

Dancers on the pavilion whirled around Raymond and Beatrice. The couple stood mute and motionless. Beatrice's face went as white as her dress. Raymond relaxed his grip.

They closed their eyes to savor the embrace. He sniffed the perfume she had dabbed behind her earlobe. She thought he was whispering nonsense in her ear.

Cocteau was incensed and tried not to watch his beloved in the arms of a woman. He could not admit to himself that actually it was the woman in the arms of Raymond.

Raymond knew that Cocteau was incensed, but he did not feel it. He felt as if he were intoxicated with sleep.

Beatrice felt excited. But unlike Raymond she did not care to luxuriate in languor. This was a ball and a ball was an escape for passion. Beatrice wanted to dance. The band began playing hot jazz. This inflamed her passion further. She broke away from the embrace and began to shimmy.

This was only her first fatal mistake.

Raymond's mood was destroyed. He watched Beatrice shimmy with revulsion. She danced faster and faster, her body looser and looser. Raymond's heart beat slower and slower.

He was about to go to Cocteau and leave the party when Beatrice suddenly stopped her dance and called out to him.

Usually Raymond did not like to be called to. Usually he was called by Cocteau and he had to respond at once. Beatrice too was calling imperatively. But he knew he could take his time in answering.

Beatrice called again: Raymond! Raymond! Raymond liked to hear his name called. Cocteau called him Bébé, even when others were present. When Raymond was not present Cocteau referred to him as M. Bébé. Raymond disliked this exceedingly but was afraid to speak out about it.

After all it was Cocteau's game to play the father to Raymond. It was only in this way that Raymond's real father would permit Raymond to live in Paris and be with Cocteau.

So Raymond was forced to suffer this indignity. But it was not the only indignity.

During such indignities Raymond would think of the literary success which was coming fast. Raymond was in a hurry to grow up and be rid of Cocteau. But for now he was playing Cocteau's games. It was necessary for that literary success to come.

Thanks to Cocteau, Raymond was a very precocious boy.

But when Beatrice called Raymond by his own name Raymond felt like a man.

Suddenly he wanted to escape the ball and Cocteau—with Beatrice.

Beatrice had already decided she would take him far away from Cocteau.

Some of Raymond's reason returned to him. He could not leave the ball with Beatrice. He instructed her to leave the pavilion first and he would follow.

'Immediately?' asked Beatrice.

Raymond's heart hardened. He told her to wait for him at a café he knew Cocteau despised.

'I see you have met that woman Hastings,' Cocteau said to Raymond after he saw her leave. 'A ridiculous woman. Her reputation is almost as impossible as her costume.'

Raymond did not reply.

An hour later he pleaded stomach-ache and joined Beatrice at the café.

It was light outside by the time Beatrice lured Raymond into her bedroom. It was not a lush boudoir but rather like a *chambre* in a seedy hotel. It was sparsely decorated. Beatrice told Raymond she traveled a lot.

'This is the only proper setting for love, anyway,' she said, touching her hand to her heart.

In the early light Beatrice looked old. She was more than twice Raymond's age. Raymond thought her hands looked as ravaged as she promised him her heart was.

'A ravaged heart is like a sore,' she told him. 'Also like a fire. The more it burns . . . the more it burns.'

Beatrice Hastings was a poetess of some repute.

Raymond had always believed emotion to be exhausting. Now Beatrice's words made him wonder. She was intoxicated with feeling. He had been exhausted earlier in the evening. He thought it had been Beatrice and her shimmy that had tired him. Now he realized it had been the presence of Cocteau, Cocteau's silent but heavy reproach, that had crushed his buoyant mood. It was only another's emotion that was exhausting.

Raymond remembered Beatrice on the divan, her eyes like dry ice, transported into a trance of ecstasy or terror. Only Beatrice knew which.

Raymond longed to burn within himself, like Beatrice. He lay down on her bed.

Beatrice lay down next to him. Her perfume floated to his nostrils. He felt surrounded, but not by the familiar flesh. He was suspended in air, in floats of scent. He thought of Beatrice in repose, of opium, of darkness. He felt the air begin to transport him into his inner depths.

Then Beatrice made her second fatal mistake.

Beatrice insisted that he take her at once. Her wounds were skin-deep and needed the healing power of Raymond's flesh. That is what she told him because that is what she thought he wanted to hear. She misunderstood the kind of ecstasy he craved.

Beatrice's heart burned far more than her body. But she believed that through the merging of two bodies occurred

242

the more magical merging of two hearts. Beatrice longed for the possession of Raymond's heart.

Her opium trances had left her terrified of belonging only to herself.

That was why in truth Beatrice had decided she was a medium. She could not bear being trapped in one body. She wanted to see the world through other eyes.

Beatrice's terror inspired her to new heights of physical passion. She tore and clawed at Raymond's body. Then she turned gentle. She covered him with kisses and caresses.

Neither her ferocity nor her tenderness moved Raymond. Her caresses left him cold. He had no desire to belong to yet another. But though his heart was cold as usual, his body responded as usual.

Though a medium Beatrice could not guess how cold his heart was. She did not sense that Raymond was thinking only of himself.

This was not what Raymond had hoped for. He was used to thinking only of himself when he was with Cocteau. With Cocteau his self was inviolable.

But what Raymond craved was to feel himself, to lose himself. He wanted to penetrate his own heart and soul.

Beatrice had failed him.

Raymond was a lazy boy. The affair with Beatrice dragged on dishearteningly. Only the secrecy of their liaison still thrilled him. But for Raymond this was only a pretense of secrecy. In his deepest thoughts he was sure that Cocteau knew.

But Cocteau knew only that Raymond was drifting away from him. He had always known of Raymond's cold heart; he had fallen in love with it. But Raymond was spending less and less time with him. He began to suspect a seduction by Brancusi. Never did his vanity permit him to suspect a love-affair with a woman.

What Raymond thought was pride in Cocteau was van-

243

ity. But unlike Raymond Cocteau possessed a warm heart and needed some vanity to protect it.

Raymond thought Beatrice vain but she was in truth desperate. She disguised her desperation by claiming it to be intensity of true feeling. She was proud of her lack of pride.

What Beatrice lacked in pride she made up for in drama. She played the part of the tempestuous mistress with abandon and at the same time precision. She had had much practice in the rôle.

But Raymond did not wish to play opposite this rôle. He suffered through her constant kisses and letters. He began arriving late for their rendezvous or not at all.

Beatrice was not a stupid woman. Her passion had not blinded her to the waning of Raymond's interest in her. On the contrary her passion was inspired by her despair that Raymond, like all her lovers, would not last long. She was stupid enough to blame her defeat on Cocteau.

Beatrice resorted to desperate tactics. She taunted Raymond's manhood. In one letter she wrote: 'Cocteau tells me you take *le rôle ignoble*.' She beseeched Raymond not to betray her in this confidence.

When he received this letter Raymond was furious. He did not know whom he hated more, Cocteau or Beatrice. He did not realize that above all he hated himself.

To Cocteau Raymond could say nothing. But he wrote to Beatrice telling her he wanted to see her.

Beatrice was ecstatic. This was what her taunting had intended to accomplish. She was finally to see her lover again. In her delirium she forgot her insult. She believed Raymond wanted to see her out of love.

At this encounter Raymond exhausted Beatrice. She fell limp with such exhaustion that Raymond thought she was asleep.

He began burrowing in her drawers. Silken underthings were thrown here and there.

Beatrice opened a languorous eye. 'What are you looking for?' she whispered.

Raymond did not reply. More silken underthings were tossed around the room. Beatrice sat up in bed wonderingly.

'Opium,' Raymond murmured.

Suddenly Beatrice thought she understood. 'I don't have any opium,' she said.

But Raymond did not want opium. He found what he was looking for. He turned to face Beatrice. In one hand he held two long stockings of black fishnet; in the other, a long black feather boa.

For the first time in their romance Beatrice was afraid of Raymond.

Without a word Raymond arranged the feather boa around Beatrice's throat and pulled it tight. Her face went white. Then he bound her legs together with fishnet.

Beatrice closed her eyes. She was still.

Raymond lay down beside her, watching. Never before had he seen Beatrice so beautiful. At the opium den she had looked beautiful, but it had been the queer beauty of the drugged. In her eyes he had glimpsed torment. Now she looked asleep, eternally at peace.

Suddenly Raymond was terrified. He was seeing Beatrice as death. But he did not crave death. He wanted only to grow up, to be a man. Did he desire Beatrice dead? Was his desire for Beatrice nothing more than necrophilia?

He bent to kiss her eyes but they did not open. He kissed her ears. Beatrice's scent rushed into him. His heart began beating wildly. No corpse could smell so warm and alive, so intoxicating. Never before had Raymond felt such desire.

He kissed her lips. At the instant his kiss awakened her he fell into deepest sleep.

Raymond received a note from Beatrice wishing him the best for the new year.

He put the letter in a secret hiding-place with the rest of her letters. This was to be her last.

Now that the romance was over Raymond was free to think of Beatrice with fondness. Her letters might help him analyze the workings of a woman's heart for his book about *le diable au corps*.

But Raymond could not help laughing at Beatrice's letters. He thought that all passion expressed baldly was passion expressed badly.

For this reason he had never forgiven Cocteau for the beating.

It had been Beatrice who had brought this about. In her desperation she had gone to see Cocteau. Cocteau was by then seething with jealousy. He had convinced himself that Raymond was betraying him with Brancusi.

But Beatrice was a far worse blow. Her confession destroyed Cocteau's vanity and thus his show of pride.

At first Raymond denied the liaison. Cocteau forced him to admit it. Raymond listened to Cocteau's words and not his heart. He thought Cocteau wanted the truth. But Cocteau wanted nothing more than a convincing lie.

Raymond admitted everything and Cocteau beat him with savage ferocity.

If it were not for Beatrice's stupidity Raymond might have returned to her, so incensed was he with Cocteau. Instead he took up with a young woman named Marie Beerbohm.

Marie was one of the Montparnasse set. She was a friend of the painter Nina Hamnett. Cocteau knew her, but thought her a little mouse. She was always very quiet.

246

He did not understand that this might appeal to Raymond very much.

When Beatrice learned of the liaison she forgave Cocteau everything and turned her venom towards this new rival. She envied Marie her legs.

But since Marie did not wear fishnet stockings, her legs did not excite Raymond.

When he took Marie as his mistress Raymond considered falling in love. In Marie he saw his perfect lover. She made no demands. She was totally submissive. Raymond did not have to drug her to see her in repose, as with Beatrice.

But Marie's body soon began to bore him. It was always quiet and still. Never did she show any spirit to subdue. Raymond began to imagine new ways in which he could not possess her. He decided that she was only physically powerless to resist him. She was keeping her soul from him. She was off in her own world.

For a week Raymond explored his new fascination. Marie was for him the mystery of the other.

After a week Raymond tired of this mystery. He decided he could not penetrate the mystery of Marie's soul because she did not possess one. She had none of Beatrice's spirit. Nothing could awaken her. She was cold and detached. She thought of nothing but the glamour of her self.

Raymond realized why Marie was no mystery. It was because she was not the other at all. She was a mirror-image of himself. They both saved their selves from another's feeling and thus felt none of their own.

Cocteau loved Raymond and so he loved Raymond's cold heart. But Raymond did not want to be like Cocteau in any way. He resolved that he would not be attracted to Marie's cold heart.

He pretended she was still his mistress only to irritate

247

Cocteau. He could not know that this was no irritation to Cocteau.

It was instead anguish.

When Beatrice's greeting heralded the new year 1922 Raymond was feeling his most passionate.

His passion was to escape from Cocteau.

In the past Raymond had planned and plotted with frustration. He knew he could not carry out his plans in cold blood.

But now his blood was hot. This passion had slowly come to a boil. Thus it was fitting that his daring escape from Cocteau happened on an impulse of the moment.

Cocteau believed Brancusi lured him away.

It was mid-January, 1922. Raymond was at a glamorous party. His mistress Marie was there. So were Picasso, Madame Picasso, Nina Hamnett, Brancusi, and Cocteau.

Only Cocteau's presence mattered to Raymond. Cocteau was the whole party.

Everyone drank champagne. It was the official opening of a new night-club, Le Boeuf sur le Toit. This Boeuf was to become the sensation of café society. Cocteau was its inspiration.

Raymond wore a white dinner jacket and drank champagne. But the champagne did not intoxicate him. The bright lights gave him a head-ache.

As if in a dream Raymond found himself leaving the party with Brancusi. They were walking Nina home to Montparnasse.

They stopped at the Dôme to buy cigarettes. 'Let's go to Marseilles,' Brancusi said.

Nina thought he was joking and declined. Raymond agreed to go. He thought about drug traffic in Marseilles. Since Marie he had given up on women. Perhaps in Marseilles he would find what he was looking for.

On the train to Marseilles Brancusi proposed going even further. They stopped in Marseilles only long enough to buy Raymond a sailor suit and then they took a boat for Corsica.

Raymond felt very gay and adventurous.

'It's just as well Nina did not come along,' Brancusi said. 'One woman isn't enough for both of us.'

Neither Raymond nor Brancusi desired Nina. She was only a good pal. This was Brancusi's subtle way of letting Raymond know that he intended to go whoring.

In Corsica the pair found several peasants and drank peasant wine. They passed two weeks in this pleasant stupor. Brancusi forgot to go whoring and Raymond forgot to look for drug-traffic. They did not forget to write to Cocteau. On the contrary Raymond would think with pleasure of Cocteau pining away with no news when everyone else in Paris had been sent postcards and telegrams. Two weeks went by before Raymond telegrammed Cocteau only to say that they might return to Paris soon and they might not.

They returned to Paris a few days later. It was not until his return that Raymond felt the exhilaration of his escape.

Cocteau received Raymond back coldly. This coldness lasted only a few days. Cocteau could forgive though he could not forget.

Raymond made sure Cocteau would not forget. All of Paris watched with diabolical curiosity* as Raymond dissipated himself with women and alcohol. But everything he did was for Cocteau.

When Cocteau took him away for their summer holiday

*On the evidence of Jacques Porel, son of the actress Réjane.

in the south Raymond was grateful. Now he could write and be by himself.

Even with Cocteau at his side Raymond found he never felt more by himself than when he was writing.

He finished *Le Diable Au Corps* quickly because it no longer interested him. This book begun in his youth Raymond now found too frenetic.

Now Raymond wanted to write his mature work. He modelled this new book on the seventeenth-century classic *La Princesse de Clèves*.

Writing this chaste story of suppressed passion excited Raymond. At night he would be so exhausted he would fall asleep dreaming of his words.

In this way the whole summer he was left alone by Cocteau.

1923

Raymond's picture appeared all over France. It was the biggest publicity campaign ever known. *Le Diable Au Corps* was an instant bestseller and Raymond its boy genius was at last a celebrity in his own right.

Finally Raymond had achieved the ambition that had driven him since childhood. This ambition had driven him to Paris and the arms of Cocteau. Now he was famous enough and rich enough to leave both.

Raymond took an austere room in a hotel near the Luxembourg Gardens that was frequented by members of the Senate. It was here that Raymond began his new life of indulgence.

Raymond did not stay often in his room. He ate sumptuous meals alone in the hotel dining-room. He would eat sole, pheasant, cheese and meringue at a sitting. He would drink coffee, liqueur, cocktails, whole bottles of champagne and wine.

Then he would go to parties and dance-halls.

It was easier for Raymond to enjoy parties and dance-halls with plenty of liquor and money.

Once he went to an opium den, hoping that in this too he would become addicted.

It was a woman who introduced Raymond to opium smoking. Her name was Madame de Warkowska and nobody in Cocteau's circle knew her. She wore a black silk samurai cloak and a white face.

Raymond met her at the Boeuf sur le Toit and disappeared with her to the den.

He felt the excitement for that which has been desired and denied for just long enough. Now he would finally smoke. His nostrils quivered in anticipation.

Madame de Warkowska led him in the dark, her slender finger pressing against Raymond's pulse point. He could not feel her touch. He enslaved all his senses to his nose.

But Madame de Warkowska did not use perfume.

She fixed a pipe for Raymond and disappeared into the darkness.

Raymond inhaled. The smell of the opium was not what he remembered. It was missing its intoxicating power.

Alone, Raymond waited for the mysteries of the laudanum to reveal themselves. He thought about Beatrice on the divan. Now he would know if she had felt the ecstasy or terror of peace. Now he would know himself.

He found himself wishing Madame de Warkowska would return. . . .

Madame de Warkowska found him asleep. 'You looked beautiful,' she told Raymond after awakening him. 'Like an angelic little boy.'

But Raymond had felt nothing. The drug had brought him nothing but sleep. He had not even had any dreams. His head ached as it always did after a long night of drinking.

Raymond had experienced nothing.

Raymond now set out to ravage the beauty of his youth. He lived fast and loose. Cocteau pleaded with him to drink milk and water.

Instead Raymond took Cocteau with him from party to party and drank until he felt loose and gay.

With Brancusi at his side Raymond revived his appetite for women. They would go to dance-halls and pick them up. Then they would dance with them.

At one dance-hall Raymond met two sisters, Bronya and Tilya Perlmutter. They were lively girls from Eastern Europe who were not yet jaded by the glamour of Paris. They were too poor to live as anything but bohemians in Montparnasse. Before Raymond they had only met sailors at the dance-hall.

Raymond found their naiveté charming. Their liveliness refreshed him. He quoted Apollinaire: 'You have to do things.'

Raymond danced and danced. He shimmied so fast he forgot everything.

But Raymond also danced very slowly, holding Bronya tightly against him, forgetting nothing. . . .

When he left for the summer holiday with Cocteau Bronya promised to write.

This summer was not like the last. Raymond and Cocteau arrived in the south alone only to be quickly joined by most of their Paris friends.

Raymond wanted most to see Georges Auric and his typewriter. The composer typed as Raymond dictated the revised version of his new masterpiece *Le Bal de Comte d'Orgel.*

No longer did Raymond write alone. He did not want to be left to himself.

Whenever he was left to himself he would drink secretly.

252

Raymond and Cocteau began writing a story in collaboration. It was a romantic story about a young girl. The girl becomes a prostitute and then falls in love. All her eagerness to be grownup disappears. She wants to return to the pure days of her youth.

Two of Raymond's drinking-companions from Paris came to visit. Raymond did not stop his secret drinking. He merely began public drinking as well.

One of these drinking-companions was an American homosexual, but he was wealthy. The other was a real *comte*. Between drinks Raymond picked this *comte*'s brains for his book. He wanted the *comte* to tell him everything there was to know about the subtleties of the French aristocracy.

He chose the charming Bolette Natanson to tell him everything she knew about women. Her words would often so inflame him that he would run off to his story. But first he would find his typist.

Thus the book progressed well. To reward himself Raymond ate oysters. He ate them often and greedily.

Raymond discovered that he shared this passion with Valentine Hugo, Jean Hugo's wife. Valentine had been courted by Cocteau years earlier.

Cocteau did not mind Valentine and Raymond eating oysters together. So what if Valentine and Raymond both loved oysters? He and Beatrice had both loved Raymond.

One day Cocteau decided to eat oysters with Valentine and Raymond. He found them oddly cold.

'You must know oysters are aphrodisiac,' said Valentine.

'No sense wasting them on you,' said Raymond.

'Ah,' Cocteau said, 'are you jealous of my past little romance with Valentine?'

Soon Cocteau and Raymond returned to Paris and Bronya came to live with Raymond in his hotel room.

Raymond continued to drink but he did not feel much

like dancing. His stomach ached. He told Bronya it was only heart-burn and refused to let her call a doctor.

Raymond enjoyed this sensation of a burning heart. He told everyone he was going to marry Bronya.

Still he would not admit that he loved her. He was marrying her only because he refused to become a 40-year-old man called Madame Jean Cocteau.

But Raymond knew he would never be a 40-year-old man.

Valentine was still travelling with her husband in the south. She was not well. Ever since her last oyster-supper with Raymond she had been suffering from fever and violent pains.

Nobody guessed that Valentine and Raymond suffered from the same ailment. Both had eaten bad oysters and had caught typhoid fever. But the disease struck each in its own way.

Raymond felt no fever at all. He was shaken with chills. Finally Cocteau sent for his doctor to treat Raymond. This doctor was reputed to be one of Paris's finest. Yet he had failed to save Apollinaire.

The doctor diagnosed pneumonia and Raymond grew worse.

Raymond did not know what he suffered from. He only knew he felt terrible.

When the real disease was discovered it was too late to save him.

Three days before he died Raymond was delirious. He told Cocteau that he was going to die in three days. Cocteau could not console him.

'There is a color moving about, with people hidden in it,' Raymond told Cocteau.

Cocteau wanted to send them all away.

'No, you can't,' Raymond told him, 'because you don't see the color.'

Did Raymond see white, in clouds and clouds of scent?

Raymond died alone, his face horribly contorted with the first pain he truly felt.

EPILOGUE

Valentine survived.

Cocteau took to opium to assuage his grief at Raymond's death.

Through the clouds of smoke he would see the white coffin and the white flowers at the funeral he did not have the courage to attend.

Brancusi told him Raymond had taken opium. Thus his opium-smoking became a mourning-ritual for Raymond.

This ritual Cocteau chose over women, oysters, and alcohol.

Cocteau would lie for hours on the divan, dreaming of Raymond so cold and untouchable beside him. . . .

Cocteau could no longer be Raymond's lover. Unwittingly he was becoming Raymond's beloved. He was now the type Raymond might have fallen in love with.

If only Raymond could have seen Cocteau, his body paralyzed by drugs and grief, in that repose so perfect that the fires of the soul are invisible. . . .